Saving

Grace

By Beverly Ovalle

Saving Grace

Imprint: Midwest Dragon Press

Copyright © 2020 Beverly Ovalle

ISBN: **978-1-952525-00-1**

First E-book Publication: March 2020

Cover: Anytime Author Promotions

Editing: Mellow Wood Editing

All cover art and logo copyright © 2020 by Beverly Ovalle

Dedication

Thank you to Robin, Diana, Josephine and Kathleen for your wonderful help as beta readers! You are always willing to answer my cry for help and I can't tell you how much that means to me.

Thank you to the 'technical team'. Anytime Author Promotions for the cover I just had to nab. Mellow Wood Editing for catching all my errors, spelling, grammar and the plot holes I could walk through.

Of course, a thank you to my family who works to find time for me to write before I do my pressure cooker gone wrong impression.

Finally, to my best friend Tamara who I miss like crazy. My sounding board, my partner in crime. If it hadn't been for her prodding I wouldn't be published. I'd still be scribbling and tossing my imagination into the trash like I did for so many years. I'll miss you forever.

TABLE OF CONTENTS

CHAPTER ONE

Lightning split the air. Storm clouds raced across the sky, bringing a never-ending stream of rain and thunder. The shadows of the flying dragons barely visible through the rain.

Rog flew through the wind farm. His wings tilted, catching gusts of wind and letting him dodge the long poles and razor-sharp blades of the windmills. Some were hanging haphazardly. Others pointed skyward, and still others burrowed deep in the ground from where they'd fallen. Burns on the blades showed evidence of previous lightning strikes. One windmill still turned in the air, blades moving in a circular motion.

Hark raced him, diving, swooping amongst the poles and avoiding the brilliant flashes of lightning. Rain pounded down, thunder rolling through the clouds.

Abandoned fields lay fallow below. Trees grew haphazardly, seeds planted by the wind or dropped by birds. Evidence of previous enclosures surrounded sections of lands, the only testament that humans once existed there.

Rivers wound through the landscape, bushes and trees lining their banks. Cattle crowded beneath their branches, huddled together. Lowing, their mournful cries echoed amongst the thunder.

Wind carried him forward, pushing him faster. His blood raced, thrumming through his veins. He dived, talons extended, snatching a cow and flying away. Rog trumpeted in triumph. Behind him, Hark bugled.

Turning his head, Rog rolled his eyes. Hark was waving a cow in each claw, showing off. His grin mocking Rog's single catch.

Whatever. He didn't have anything to prove, especially not to Hark.

They continued flying, the lowing of the cattle in their grasps continued.

Spying a flat surface, black and crumbling, Rog circled, then landed. Hark as usual followed.

Settling down, Rog feasted. The warmth of flesh and crunchy bones filling his belly. Nothing but the sounds of their feeding filled the air. Even the insects knew a predator when they saw one. Of course, it could be the rain and lightning. He preferred to think it was them.

Hark burped, flame slipping out.

"Watch it." Rog spat a burst of flame back.

"Pfft. You know it won't hurt you." Hark rolled over on his back. "What do you think humans used this for?"

"It's a road of some sort. I'm not sure what they needed such a fancy one for." Rog looked around. "It doesn't seem like they even finished it."

Surrounding them, equipment stood, metal pieces crisscrossing into the air. Cables hung down, attached to long metal forms. Columns stood nearby, standing, solid forms of stone reaching into the sky with nothing on them.

"If they only knew what would happen, do you think they would have built so many useless things?" Hark twisted, scratching his back against the loose stone on the ground.

Rog shrugged, looking around. "Maybe. Humans do many useless things."

Hark rolled, settling on his stomach against the black. "It is warm, though."

Rog wiggled, stretching next to him. The warmth of the black stone seeping into his belly. "It is. It may be useless to the humans, but I like it."

The storm continued to rage above them. The cool rain splashed off his scales running off him to the sides of the road. Opening his mouth, Rog rolled out his tongue capturing drops and swallowing them.

"Do you think we will ever find our mates?"

Rog glanced over at Hark. His brother was once again on his back, jaws open, swallowing rain. "Yes. When they need us or we get near them. I'm not sure which."

"Do you feel a pull? Like our dam said?" Hark shifted to his side, looking at him.

"No." Rog glanced around the wilderness surrounding them. "I think maybe it's not our turn yet." He yawned, his jaw cracking. "Maybe our sisters will find their mates first."

"Yeah. I don't want to be tied down yet. Look at how Ari and Crag are tied to their mates' apron strings." His wistful tone belied his words. Hark dropped his head down, laying against the surface.

"Me either." Rog doubted Hark believed him either. It was hard leaving their brothers and their mates. Both women were spitfires and Ari and Crag were wrapped around their dainty fingers. With both women expecting, they were busy settling in to the weyr their brothers created over the years.

In addition, the rescued ice dragons, all still considered children and adolescents in dragon years were creating a frenzy amongst the new weyr and the old. Everyone wanted to make sure they survived and the ensuing spoiling of the dragonettes had gotten out of hand.

Crag even ignored the fact one of them had stolen his mate. Even if it was to save them all, Rog wasn't sure he'd be so understanding. But Faith wasn't his mate and he was glad of it. Glad there were no more sisters to snag him or Hark.

With the fire dragons, and his newly mated brothers, he and Hark were able to get away. Rog wanted to see the world around them, see the changes and fly free. Hark followed, a grin on his face when they flew away after a short goodbye.

They'd flown far away from the mountains their family laid claim to. Across flat plains and after months of exploring, they'd reached more mountains. Smaller than the ones they grew up in. More wooded. But with the knowledge of fire dragons they knew deep below these mountains lay a volcano. One that would hatch eggs and warm dragons.

Stretching, the rain washing away any dirt on his scales, Rog settled down. He felt like a nap and decided this was as good a time as any.

"Gonna nap." Rog yawned.

"'Kay." Hark didn't object.

Rog never thought he would. His brother had two speeds, full speed ahead or dead stop. Rarely did Rog see anything else when they were together. Around the other dragons, especially the new mates, his brother seemed like a different dragon.

Rog wiggled, moving toward the edge of the road. It actually turned into a bridge just a few feet over. Too lazy to get up, he squirmed until he was on the bridge portion. The black wasn't as warm here. Shimmying just a bit more, Rog was able to look down.

He sputtered, shaking his head. Lowering it again, expecting the water this time, he drank. Gulping in enough to quench his thirst, Rog shimmied back to the surface, laying his head down. The rain he swallowed earlier, had only made him thirstier.

Hark bumped his side. "Water? Move over a bit."

Rog pulled his legs under himself and scuttled sideways, making room. "Yes."

"I wonder if there are any fish?" Hark leaned beneath the bridge, rearing back shaking his head. "You could have warned me it was so close." He laughed, going back under.

Curious, Rog turned around. On the other side of the bridge, there was no water, just grass. Circling around again, he stuck his head back in the water. Opening his eyes, leaving the bottom lid covering his eyes for protection, Rog looked around.

The water, greenish blue, was clear. Hark was right. There were fish. The water, darker under the bridge appeared to go underground before coming back up a bit further away. Cold. Rog shivered. The temperature crept under his scales, giving him microscopic goosebumps along his tough, leathery skin.

Leaning further, Rog dug his talons into the surface, following the water down with his head, stretching his neck. Just flowing water.

Rearing back, Rog whipped his head, shaking the water from his scales. Shivering, tremors rolled under his scales, dispelling the last of the water from beneath them.

"Brr." Rog moved, finding a smooth spot on the black road, away from the bridge and settled down. The warmth of the surface calming the prickling of his scales and skin. "Feels like it came straight from a glacier."

Hark shook his head, sparkling drops of water spraying around him. "I think you're right."

Looking around, Rog didn't spy any mountains, none he would consider mountains at any rate. Nothing he thought would lend itself to making the water so cold. "Maybe underground caverns."

Hark nodded. Following Rog's example, he proceeded to find a warm spot, circling until he rested against the surface. "Now for that nap."

Rog concurred. Belly against the warmth, he drew his feet beneath him, curled his head and tail around himself and closed his eyes. Relaxing, he slowly sank into a deep slumber. After all, who would disturb two dragons?

***

Grace kept tabs on the creatures flying over her herd. Hiding in the trees along the river, she glared, watching them steal away her cattle. Sure, it was probably enough to feed them and no more, but those were hers.

Observing them, she shrugged her aggravation away. They were just as much animals as the cows. Circle of life and all that. She wondered if they were really dragons. One of the books that she read showed pictures of them. They seemed similar, but the book said they weren't real.

But Grace's eyes and mind were open to more than she'd ever thought. Things no one thought were real, were. Her family said it was her imagination. Fairies were real, she was positive of it, but her family called them insects. Werewolves and dragons would just bring more ridicule down on her head. Just because she spotted dragons didn't mean there were actually werewolves too.

She shivered, wrapping her arms around herself. Even with the unexpected, Grace preferred to be out here alone. Being the youngest, her family treated her like a slave. Get this, Grace. Do that, Grace. Like no one else was capable. Or they totally ignored her. Escaping to watch over the cattle became a respite. The tent they dispatched with her pathetically kept out neither the wind or rain. Grace knew she needed some place sturdier to live, more permanent.

Searching deeper in the library, she'd found a book on building. Most of it worthless for her, but the older technics showed her how to build a Soddy. Painstakingly Grace followed the instructions. She didn't need a huge place. Enough to sleep and eat and get out of the rain. Slowly she moved the most interesting books there. Books on building, raising cattle, herbs and spices, and even a few serving no practical purpose but to entertain her.

None of her family knew it was there. Built past the fields where the cattle were, her Soddy hid in plain sight. She faced it away from the path her relatives always took. To them, it was just another hill. Since the cattle were kept so far from their settlement, Grace began to spend more time there. One of her brothers or cousins would come grab a cow to butcher when meat ran low. She'd been basically living here for the past five years on her own. Going home just enough to keep them from questioning her.

Smiling, Grace thought of her accomplishment. The time passed so quickly. She remembered scouting out ruins, finding tools, rusted and unused, then carefully restoring them. Taking and hiding them beneath her tent. Once she'd found what she could, she began to work. It took her a few months, but she'd done it. Standing tall, excitement buzzing to her toes, her heart filled with joy. Her own home. It still sent a thrill through her almost five years later.

With care, she'd cut up what she needed from downed trees. Creating a bed frame and using slats instead of rope to hold up her mattress. It was a soddy. Sometimes water would seep in and this way she didn't have to sleep on a wet or moldy bed. Cured leather filled with grasses and herbs made up her mattress. She even had a pillow filled with feathers.

Grace left nothing on the floor except her bed frame. Once her bed was built, and tired of mud between her toes each morning, she decided to see what she could do about it. The remains of a road ran a couple of days away. Rock and asphalt scattered all over.

Finding a cart, one she could maneuver over the grass, called a wheelbarrow according to her books, she took the rock pieces that were as flat as possible and pushed them back to her soddy.

Then the digging began. A couple of weeks later, Grace had a floor. Her walls were still mostly mud. The one by her bed wooden. Cutting downed logs and nailing them to her soddy's frame in that section. It was too hard, and awkward to do her whole house. But she didn't want dirt falling on her while she slept.

Finding the wheelbarrow was a god send. The ruins had an old iron stove in a fallen down barn. Grace was grateful she was small. Her size let her wiggle in and out of places no one else could reach. Piece by piece she'd carted it back. Small, but strong, Grace never backed down when she made up her mind. And she wanted that stove.

The first time she'd lit it, the smoke chased her out of her home. Once the pile of twigs burned out, she'd gone back in, frustrated at the mess. Her soddy was warm from the stove, but now the floors and walls were coated in a mess of ash inside. Not that it made a difference with the mud walls. With a few trial and error experiences, she finally got it fixed. She managed a vent from discarded pieces of piping from the ruins and scrounged from her family's homestead.

A small counter kept her books safe and gave her room to prepare meals. The little stove had a small spot to cook on. Another discarded pan, a little beat up, and missing a handle, found in the rubble of the old buildings worked for her. She had a couple of ducks for eggs. Sneaking in the nests she'd found, Grace grabbed a few eggs and hatched them. Feeding them kept the ducks coming back. Soon enough, they were laying eggs. Enough for her.

Grace knew there was no way to sneak any chickens from her family. A strict breeding program accounted for every egg and chicken. It was her family's main source of food besides the massive gardens, but every family had those.

Finding the herd and growing it, adding to the pantry for everyone helped her status. She'd even finished a small smoker. Plenty of stones and scrap metal to smoke the meat. She rarely used the cattle, just rabbits, squirrels and anything else caught in her traps for her own use. Back with her family, they had a smokehouse to help preserve the meat.

"Well, time to explore, Gracie girl." Sometimes she needed to hear a voice, even if it was her own. Grabbing a knife, bow and arrow set, walking stick, backpack and canteen, Grace headed out.

The weather was getting colder and over the winter months she liked to see what she could find and fix. Plus, she needed to check her traps. She didn't want to admit her curiosity about the creatures who stole some of the cattle.

Slamming her door, wedging it shut to keep out any stray critters, Grace headed toward the river and filled her canteen with fresh water. Looking into the sky, she wondered if she should even go. The rain didn't seem to want to let up. But sometimes the force of the water would uncover items she could use. Swinging a waterproofed cape around her, tying it in front, she looked again to the sky. Pulling on her hat, covering her ears, Grace figured she was as dry as she could get.

Her backpack had a couple days' worth of food, enough for her planned destination. She'd been planning on this trip for a couple of weeks. Knowing the rain would bring snow, Grace wanted to see if she could salvage more from the abandoned mines and shacks that were in ruins there.

Her family rarely came this way, having dismissed the worth of any items there. Grace read her books and learned how to use the smallest scrap to make her life better. Admittedly it was because there was so little to go around. However, she enjoyed the sense of accomplishment it gave her.

Gazing once more at the sky, Grace left. She headed in the direction the creatures flew. Ignoring that fact, she followed a familiar path and headed into the hills. The man-made caves held items she could usually use. Plus, it would get her out of the rain. If she happened to spy dragons, well, what could it hurt?

Surely, they were smart enough to get in out of the rain?

CHAPTER TWO

Rog yawned and stretched. Toes and talons wiggling, legs straight out in front and behind him, Rog worked out his kinks. Next to him, Hark burped, snorted, and woke up. Charming.

"Now what?" Rog stretched his spine. He grunted with each pop. Wriggling to check for any stiffer spots, he lay splayed out, relaxed, finding none.

"I could eat again." Hark stuck his head over the bridge. "I want some fish." The words were muffled by the water.

Rog rolled his eyes, but joined his brother anyway. He could eat. The cold water pebbled up his skin, causing his scales to stand up. He closed his first lid, protecting his eyes. He opened his jaws, letting the water run into his mouth and down his jaw. He waited. His tongue started freezing. Snapping his jaw shut, Rog shook, jumping back up onto the surface.

Looking at Hark, sitting in the river, blocking all but the water Rog realized why no fish got through. The hog was taking all of them.

Spinning around, Rog swatted Hark with his tail. *Don't be such a pig.* Sometimes it was easier to speak mind to mind.

Hark slapped his tail down, chortling as water coated Rog.

Rog shivered. The water was so cold. It didn't seem to bother Hark. Rog would prefer to cuddle up to a warm body... No, he couldn't go there. He wasn't ready for a mate.

"This water is just too cold. I want to see where it's coming from." Rog stood up, looking at the winding river. It appeared to gradually head uphill. "Do you want to explore with me?"

"Sure. Here, catch." Hark tossed a mess of fish, hitting him in the face. They flopped around on the grass, covered in slime and now dirt and grass.

"Thanks." Rog stopped thinking about it and gobbled them up. His stomach growled, wanting more. More he got.

Hark tossed more, more water and more fish. "I heard that grumbling. Eat up. You should've eaten another cow earlier."

Rog ignored him, slurping up the offering. Sure, he should have, but his stomach was full then. He had no desire to fatten up like his brother Crag. That dragon could practically drag his belly when he walked. Of course, his mate, Faith, didn't seem to mind.

Another mess of fish hit his head. "Okay, that's enough." Rog quickly ate them, rinsing his face and front limbs in the river. "Thank you. Ready?"

Hark nodded, climbing up the bank. Shaking his body while he walked. He glanced up. "Do you think the rain will stop anytime soon?"

Rog looked at the sky. While it wasn't as dark as a few hours ago, it still looked drab. "No. It looks pretty miserable. Maybe we can find a cave or something. Get a fire going."

"Sounds great." Hark lumbered along, walking beside Rog. "Want to fly?"

Rog had been thinking the same thing. "Yeah. Why walk when we have wings?"

Grinning at each other, they burst into a run, wings flapping, gaining altitude at the same time.

"Beat you." Rog trumpeted into the air.

"Nope. I beat you." Hark rolled, grinning back at him.

"Tied."

"Fine. Tied."

They followed the river. It led up into the hills. Deceptively simple, Rog was sure walking would be more trouble than expected if they had gone that way. Rocky surfaces shown through the grass. More and more rock.

"I'm sure we'll find caves. Look at all the rock."

Rog flew, turning away from the river, climbing higher. He frowned. He felt almost driven.

Hey, I thought you wanted to follow the river. Hark looked at the river and back to Rog.

I do, I did. Something is pulling me this way. Hurry. It feels urgent. Rog didn't wait. He flew in the direction his heart was tugging him.

You know what this means. Your mate is somewhere this way.

And she's in trouble. Hurry. Rog pumped his wings, catching a current, speeding faster.

Hark followed.

Regardless of what either of them said, they wanted a mate. But having a mate in trouble, one you hadn't even met was harrowing. Rog flew, faster than ever. He let his heart lead. No wonder his brother Ari seemed tense before he met his mate Hope.

Of course, Hope was wonderful. A small spitfire, and Rog watched over her when Ari wasn't around. But their PDA could be too much sometimes. His urge to fly the coop, so to speak, and spread his wings across the continent became too much to pass up. With his normal partner in crime, Hark, also footloose and fancy free, they headed out. Flying east to see the vast country they were in.

Reigning his mind back to now, panic struck Rog, upsetting his flight. Recovering, his breath coming in sharp pants, he banked. Circling the area, trying to arrow in on the fear filling him. The hills, rocks and trees made spotting anything on the ground difficult.

The pain and panic were here. Somewhere. His mate was here and she needed saving, or help. *She's here somewhere. She's in pain. See if you can see her.*

Hark headed back. He'd outpaced Rog and returned to help Rog search. *I'll circle opposite. Just to make sure we don't miss her.*

Thanks. Rog closed his eyelids, letting the emotions in his heart and gut guide him. Shaking his head, he opened them. He knew he was close, but nothing pinpointed exactly to where she was. He dove closer to the mountain. She could be in any number of nooks or crannies. The rain turned everything a shade of gray.

A movement caught his eye. He arrowed in on it. He dropped his head, wings drooping. Trash blowing in the wind, anchored to a bush and waving wildly. Not her.

Here, I think I see something or someone over here.

On my way. Rog flew toward his brother's location. His breath caught. Hanging upside down, foot caught in a tree branch was… He cocked his head. A body. He dove closer. It was moving. Face obscured by a cloth hanging down and struggling. Her swinging body looked treacherously close to slipping. A hand reached out at each swing to try to catch the tree. Lack of reach or perhaps the ever-present rain prevented her from reaching her goal.

Rog swooped in, grabbed her in his talons. Pulling her from the tree, he flew up toward a ledge. He tightened his grasp at her struggle. He set her down on the ledge, landing beside her.

Hark landed next to him.

Before she had a chance to scream, and they always did, he shifted into his human form.

Hark looked at him and did the same.

She shivered, jaw dropping and began to sway. Her eyes rolled to the back of her head. Rog leaped forward to catch her.

***

Grace swung from a branch, thinking she'd caught a glimpse of the dragons again. Moving to the edge of the rock to check, her feet slipped. Grabbing anything she could to prevent falling down into the gully, her foot caught in a tree. Wedging into a vee of a tree branch. Heart in her throat, and her pulse beating in her ears, Grace tried to swing enough to catch another branch of the spindly, pathetic tree she'd fallen into.

Her rain cape hampered her efforts. She didn't want to lose it by removing it, so she batted it away from her head when she grabbed at the tree. Wind battered her and then something grabbed her, pulling her away.

Oh God, it had to be a dragon. Not that she could see. Her damn cape still covered her head and face. She didn't have long to panic before she felt solid ground beneath her. Struggling to stand, she uncovered her face.

Heart racing, Grace screamed. She couldn't back away. The ledge she'd already fallen off of was behind her. She swore the dragon winced at the sound. Another landed beside him. Then, before her eyes, he changed into a man. They both did.

Grace goggled at them. Her limbs melted and her vision narrowed and darkened.

Arms surrounded her. Warm and firm, Grace just wanted to snuggle closer. Remembering why she was laying on the ground she stilled.

"What are you?" Her voice trembled despite her best efforts. But, heck, she was scared. If this man really was a dragon, she'd seen him lift a cow with no effort and fly away. There was no doubt in her mind he ate it. What would he do with her? She'd make an appetizer. A pitiful one at that.

"I'm a dragon shifter." His voice poured over her like honey, smooth and rich.

Her belly tightened and the hair on the back of her neck stood on end while goosebumps ran along her body. Maybe this is how he attracted his prey. Being so attractive he pulled you in under his spell.

"Okay." She'd never heard of such a thing. But she'd seen it with her own eyes. "Can you do that anytime you want?" Her legs trembled, her whole body did. Her breathing hadn't settled down since she slipped off the ledge.

"Sure." One minute he was a man and the next a dragon. Then he shifted back again. "What do you think?"

Stunned, her mind ran in circles. Nothing stood out except this man was a predator. Even his eyes showed it. Yellow, the purest gold stared back at her. She reflexively took another step back, jerking to a halt when he grabbed and pulled her toward him.

Her stomach twisted when she remembered the drop.

He'd saved her again. His hands held hers. Heat enveloped her. He radiated an insane amount of heat.

Chilled, she stepped closer. Maybe he wasn't going to eat her. Her eyes flicked toward the other man, dragon, dragon shifter. He stood there, looking bored, checking out the entrance to the mine behind them.

"This would be a good place to hole up." The other man's voice was deep but didn't roll across her skin like hot butter. "I'm Hark by the way." He waved and walked into the mine. Presumably to investigate.

"I'm Rog. What's your name?" He seemed a bit formal, his speech a bit stilted. He grabbed a small bag from his shoulder, pulling out pants and a shirt and quickly dressing.

"Grace." Her tensed muscles relaxed. If they were exchanging names, hopefully she would be safe. At least from being their next meal. Two men alone with her, in a deserted mine presented another problem, but he did get dressed. "Are you two related?"

"Brothers." Rog nodded. "Shall we get in out of the rain?" He waved toward the mine. "I presume this cave is where you were headed. Or were you leaving?"

Wringing her hands, she slipped around him. "Coming to the mine. I try to salvage what I can." Maybe she was crazy, but she didn't think they meant her any harm. Her heart slowed and her breathing started to even out. Her skin still twitched a bit, and goosebumps still presented on her arms, but she'd been cold from the rain.

Crossing the ledge and ducking in the mine, the tremor in her limbs increased. Her wet clothes and the mine temperature were too much. Maybe she should have stayed home.

A crackle and the smell of smoke caught her attention. Hark busily started a fire, using the huge logs that once upon a time ran under the rails. He too had put on clothes, though both men still were barefoot. Hark shot flame from his mouth to start it.

Grace jumped back in surprise. So, yeah, maybe she should have expected that. But, whoa, she hadn't. She supposed being part dragon gave them strength she hadn't expected. She'd never been able to lift the logs. And the fire. Not like she'd ever imagined dragons, let alone dragon shifters.

A smile slipped across her face, the heat welcome. Grace hurried over to the fire, her shivering body demanding warmth. If she'd been alone, she'd have bundled up in a blanket she stored there. With two unknown... men... she didn't dare. If they hadn't thought about harming her, she wasn't going to give them the idea.

"Thank you. I've never been able to use the wood. I can't lift it."

Hark nodded. "Dragon shifters are strong. One of our advantages."

Grace took off her rain cape and hung it from a nail in one of the tresses. She noticed Hark built the fire in the same spot she usually did. As innocuous as they seemed, Grace needed to remember they were predators. More cunning than most, she'd bet.

Rog came near, just off to her side.

She knew because the hair on her arms stood up. Grace didn't even have to look at him to know. This one affected her. The feelings he aroused were unlike anything she'd felt before. Certainly, none of the men at home. Most of them were related in one way or another. Too closely she felt.

"That feels good." Rog stepped just a bit closer to the fire.

Grace almost put her hands out to stop him from getting too close but stopped herself. Dragon. She bet the fire wouldn't affect him at all.

"Ever since I immersed myself in the river, I've been cold. This is just what I've needed." He sighed. "I want to just step into it to warm myself to my bones." He ran his hands up and down his arms. The shiver followed the friction.

She knew how he felt. She'd been cold for the last week. The never-ending rain penetrated everything. She preferred the snow. It, at least, provided insulation. But it was too early for snow and too late in the season for the summer heat. The trees were already turning colors. Soon they would fall, creating a mess. Her garden would need to be harvested soon before the root crops decayed in the rain.

She mentally shook herself. She should be worried, being here with two men she didn't know. Not letting her mind wander. They made her feel comfortable. Like she'd known them a while. Knowing they were animals, she should be running away from them. Not standing around a fire enjoying the heat. Enjoying the heat from Rog and the fire he kindled in her body.

They weren't even the same species. She glanced at Rog from the corner of her eye, not that you'd know it looking at him now.

"I'm hungry." Hark looked around like he expected food to be right there waiting for him to notice.

"So, go hunt. Bring back enough for all of us." Rog stepped closer to the fire.

"Not my cattle." He needed to know. Her family couldn't afford to lose more. If what they grabbed earlier was only a meal, they'd ruin them in a week.

Hark looked at me. "Your cattle?"

"Yes. I saw you take them earlier. My family needs them to survive." Grace glared at him.

"A couple wouldn't be noticed." He moved subtlety, trying to intimidate her.

"You've already had a couple." Oh hell no. She'd put up with enough of that to last a life time. She'd squirmed out from under her family's thumb. She wouldn't allow some man, dragon, to put her under someone else's. "Go over the hills. There are wild cattle there. Plus, real big ones. Buffalo my books call them."

Hark perked up. "Bigger than normal? I'll go check it out." He turned, left the tunnel.

She could hear the subtle change of the sound of the rain, beating against wings instead of the soft pitter pat against the dirt and rock. A breeze blew back into the mine, then the dragon lifted off and flew away.

Grace's jaw dropped. She stared. Amazed at the sight of the giant creature. "I can't believe that's real." She looked at Rog. "You're really dragons."

A crooked smile crossed his face. "Yes. We're really dragons."

"Aren't you afraid of getting shot."

"Not too many guns left around."

Grace snorted. "Don't bet on it. My family has them. And they use them to hunt. It's how I know about the buffalo."

"Hmm. We thought most of the humans had died. We haven't found a lot of them while we fly around the country."

Grace shrugs. "We've been here for a long time. Generations. Before the apocalypse I think."

"Where is the rest of your family?"

"At home. I take care of the cattle. I pretty much moved here and they didn't really seem to notice." She snorts. "They think I live in that pathetic tent they gave me. I've been here years."

"You don't? Where do you live then? Here?"

"No." She laughed. "I built a soddy. You can't see if you don't know it's there."

Rog frowned. "What is a soddy?"

Grace smiled. "It's a home built from mud bricks and the roof is sod. Grass, so it blends in. There was a small hill, perfect really. I dug into it, hollowed it out and began reinforcing it." She thought for a second. "A mud cave, really. I've found a stove to heat the place, fixed it up and put it in. I even put in a stone floor. I got tired of muddy feet."

"And your family thinks you live in a tent?" Rog's eyes were big, listening to her.

She puffed up in pride. "Yup. Can you believe that? Like I could have survived out here in winter in a tent." She shook her head, sighing. "I don't know if they're stupid or they just don't care."

"I'd love to see it." Rog's eyes shined in the mine. Maybe too much so.

Grace fought down a shiver. The reflective shine caught her by surprise. For a moment, he'd seemed so normal. She could almost believe he was a man. One that twisted up her stomach and made it ache. One that sent her heart racing and pulse thumping and then he looked at her like he could eat her. Her heart raced in fear or excitement. She wasn't really sure.

CHAPTER THREE

He stared at Grace, not moving a muscle. Her scent wafted between arousal and fear. He wasn't sure she knew what arousal was. Fear, she knew too well. Each time, her body tensed, wanting to run but knowing that showing weakness to a predator would get her killed.

Not so, in this case.

"I'm not going to hurt you." He kept his voice low, even. He wanted to reassure her, but wasn't quite sure how. Time would prove it to her. He just didn't know how much time she'd give him.

Grace looked down, toward the fire. She didn't believe him. "Good." She nodded, not looking at him. "That's good."

Rog sighed. Maybe he shouldn't have shown her he was a shifter. But he'd seen how poorly springing it on his brother's mates went. A chuckle burst from him. Maybe Hark could get it right.

Grace's head swung back up. She stared at him. "What's so funny?"

"When my brothers, Ari and Crag, met their mates, they didn't tell them they were dragon shifters. It scared the hell out of them when they met their dragons. I swore I would be upfront. Let her know what I was." He looked Grace in the eye. "I'm not going to hurt you. I couldn't hurt you."

"Are you saying, I'm your mate? What is that even?" Grace gave him a look, leaving him in no doubt she didn't believe one word coming from his mouth.

"I found you because you were in danger. My heart, my gut, my soul brought me here. I know you are my mate." Rog stepped forward, grabbing her hands. A sizzle shot up his arms.

Grace's startled expression showed she felt the shock too. She struggled to pull her hands away from him.

Rog just held on tight. "A mate is the other half of a soul. Fate draws a dragon to his heart and soul. As it did for me. Bringing me to you." He spoke with all the passion he could muster. She had to believe him.

Grace frowned. "Okay." She sighed, tugging on her hands. "So, you won't hurt me." Shaking her head, she glanced at the fire. "The rest sounds a bit farfetched. Of course, I did see you change from a dragon to a man. And you can do it whenever you want?"

Rog nodded. He decided it was a rhetorical question.

"But you can't prove you won't hurt me."

He shook his head.

"Well then." She tugged her hands again. "Let go of me."

Rog dropped her hands. He hoped she didn't reject him. He didn't know what he'd do if she did. But she was human. She'd need time to accept his words, and only time would prove himself.

He squared his shoulders. Fate couldn't be wrong. He would give her what she needed, even if it meant waiting for what he desired.

Grace moved away.

He missed her warm hands and the tingle they sent through his body. He started to reach for her and stopped. Maybe she just needed to get to know him.

"Why were you up here?" Rog shoved his hands in his pockets.

"You finally asked." She slanted him a sideways look. "Winter's coming. Sometimes I find things here in the mine I can use, so I collect them and work on them when it's better to stay inside."

"Like what?"

Grace shrugged. "Depends what I find."

Rog gazed around the tunnel, walking around, curious about a manmade mine. "What have you found?"

"A wheelbarrow, an axe, a pickaxe, a couple of shovels. There are lots of metal rails and these big logs that run under them." Grace touched her foot to one log. "Lanterns, but I don't really need them. I use candles."

"Do they still have glass in them? They would be safer and light a room up better."

"Don't know. I suppose it's worth it. I never really worried about it." Grace moved a little closer to the fire, putting her hands above the flames to warm them.

"Hark might be a while. Would you like to explore?"

Grace nodded. "I'll just light a couple of candles." She pulled a couple from her backpack, lighting them in the fire. "Here, you can take one." She handed Rog one of the lit candles.

"Great. Where do you remember seeing the lanterns? I'd like to see if they would help. Especially here where there is virtually no wind." Rog turned away from the entrance, looking into the darker part of the cave. He didn't need the candle. He could see well enough in the dark, but knew that Grace needed the light.

"They were this way." Holding her candle out in front of her, she led the way deeper underground.

They stopped sooner than Rog expected. Just around the bend, a small area had been carved out. Supplies lined the shelves. Buckets, shovels, pickaxes in varying states of decay. In addition, there were other tools that Rog couldn't identify. Many of them appeared to be battery operated. The corrosion on them testified they were inoperable.

He watched Grace poke around, muttering under her breath. "Here." She leaned down and grasped something in her hand. Raising it into the air, she showed it to Rog.

"Good. Let's see if we can find any supplies for it." He skirted the piles on the floor, coming to her side. "The glass is intact. Maybe there will be wicks and fuel here."

They looked. Rog found the remnants of wicks, threads, really. Nothing they could use.

Shoving around the debris, Rog uncovered a few containers marked Kerosene. The containers appeared fine. The heavy plastic still intact. Shaking it, Rog could hear sloshing.

"It appears they still have fuel in them." Rog shook it, letting Grace hear.

"I didn't know anything was in them." Grace frowned. "Do you think it is still good?"

"Only one way to find out." Rog grabbed a couple of the containers. "Grab a couple of lanterns, as many as you can carry."

"Before we do, can you look at something I found?"

"What is it?" He hadn't noticed Grace picking up anything in particular.

"There is a door back here." Grace walked further into the room. "One that I've never been able to open. I found it, behind stuff piled up against it. It looked like it had been hidden."

Rog came over, checked the door, grabbed the padlocks examining them.

"Do you think you could open them?" Grace's body heat soaked into his back. Leaning against him, she peered around his arm. Poking at the locks.

He winced, the clang of metal against metal echoing in his ears. "I should be able to." He didn't want to say it, but afraid of hurting her, he did. "Grace, step back. I don't know how much force I'll need to use."

Her eyes glistened with excitement. She hopped back. "Is this far enough?" She watched him eagerly.

"Step back into the main area. Just in case." He preferred to err on the side of caution.

"Okay." She moved further back giving him enough room.

The door once had lettering on it but it's now faded into obscurity. Flecks of paint the only clue to show there once was writing there.

Rog heard grunting, and something large being dragged into the mine. *Is that you? What did you catch?*

I got a couple of buffalo. Mean things, and boy could they run. Not as fast as me, but still impressive. Hark grunted with each sentence.

Come back this way when you're done. There's a locked door back here. Grace found it hidden. Rog glanced at Grace, his heart racing at the sight of her.

I'll be right there.

A loud thud echoed from the entrance.

Grace jumped, looking back toward the noise.

"It's just my brother. He's back from hunting." Rog turned back to the door. "He caught a couple of buffalo."

"I didn't hear him."

***

"We can talk to each other telepathically." Rog tugged on the center lock, letting it fall back down. The harsh clang rang in her ears.

"You mean, like, mind to mind?" Grace's jaw dropped. Crazy talk, she thought, but no crazier than a dragon changing into a man.

Rog grunted, pulling on the lock. The groan of metal met her ears. "Yes."

She watched his arms bulge, his back muscles defined in the soft shirt he wore. They strained, his muscles firm. His thighs tight in the pants, showing off his strength.

A shriek of metal and a sharp snap sounded. The clunk of the lock hit the ground and Rog's muscles softened.

"That's one lock done." Rog reached for another.

Two locks, one on the top, one on the bottom, were left. Even with a crowbar she hadn't been able to break them. Rog's strength was amazing. His arms stretched, pulling the metal locks apart with apparent ease. She sighed, watching him.

He flashed her a grin over his shoulder.

Heat crept up her cheeks. Grace, glanced at the ground, flustered. She never acted this way.

Rog pulled apart the last lock. He tugged on the door. It didn't budge. He banged on the hinges. A bit of dust came from them. A few flakes of paint drifted down. He tugged on the handle, muscles bulging.

"Here, move a bit." Hark grabbed her shoulders, moving her over a bit. "Looks like you need some real strength." He posed, flexing his arms. "Real muscles." He waggled his eye brows in Grace's direction.

Rog chuckled and rolled his eyes. He stepped back from the door. "Be my guest."

Hark flexed again, stepping forward. He grabbed the door and pulled. Tugged. Swore and threw his back into it.

Grace watched his muscles, sleek and defined, moving and working. She admired the view, but there was no twisting stomach, thrumming heart or shaky breathing involved. Not like watching Rog.

"I think it will take both of us." Rog stepped forward, grasping the bar on the door along with Hark.

Grace stepped back. If they got the door open, they would fly backwards. No matter how much she felt like running a hand up Rog's muscles, she didn't want to do it from the floor of the mine.

Both men grunted, pulling on the handle. Strain written in every muscle, they tugged. A low groan of metal met their ears.

A load snap and the muffled sound of metal clattered to the ground. The door swung open. Both men staggered back.

Grace frowned. There was nothing on this side. Looking at the door, it appeared to have been barred from the inside. "That's odd."

"What do you mean?" Rog picked himself up, offering a hand to his brother.

"The door was barred from the inside." Grace stepped forward, intending to pass through the door.

Rog held an arm up, blocking her. "Wait. Let me go first. Who knows what we'll find? Or who." He stepped in front of her. "Hark, take the rear."

Hark nodded, eyes gleaming. He waited behind Grace, bouncing on his toes. The eagerness for adventure oozing from every pore.

Rog peered through the door.

Grace looked from beneath his arm. He still blocked her, like he thought she'd dart ahead of him. He didn't know her that well. It was dark in there. Her candle barely lit past the door. What Grace did see didn't impress her. Dust covered the floor. Spiderwebs coating the ceiling and walls.

"Ugh." Her nose wrinkled. The smell of must tickling her nose. "I don't see a thing."

"But it's kind of curious. A locked door and yet, it was secured from the inside." Rog looked just as eager as his brother to explore.

Grace shivered. The other side of the door seemed creepy. She worried what would happen. Rog was right. It was definitely odd. Looking from Rog to Hark, Grace straightened her spine and urged Rog forward.

"You're right. It is curious. Let's find out why." Nodding her head, Grace followed. One hand holding her torch and one clamped onto Rog's arm, she shuffled forward.

"Wait. Let's use a lantern." Hark turned around. "I see you found them and fuel."

"But no wicks." Grace turned, waiting.

"We don't even know if the kerosene will light." Rog leaned against the door. "It's so old."

"We can at least try." Hark pulled off the glass cover, unscrewed the lantern top, lifting it off. He poured the sluggish fuel in. Taking part of his shirt, he ripped a scrap off, soaking it in the fuel. He tucked it up, turning a key on the side to pull the piece up. Screwing the top back on, he looked up. "Here, light the cloth."

Grace touched the torch to the wick, jumping when the flame caught with a whoosh. "Guess it still works."

Hark pulled down the glass, adjusted the key and the flame steadied.

"It does light better." The glow emanated in an even ring around Hark.

"Good. Leave the candles here. I think the lantern would be safer. Less chance of a wind in the tunnels blowing it out."

"What if the flame goes out?" Grace didn't want to be left in the dark. She was pretty sure the men could see in the dark. They moved too easily around any debris to not see it.

"Uh, fire dragons. I am the flame." Hark's teeth shown in a huge, cheeky grin.

Rog wasn't the only one rolling his eyes.

"What if the fuel runs out?" She wondered how he'd answer.

"I'm sure there is something to use as a torch in the tunnel." Rog interjected. "Let's get rolling."

"I'd rather have the candles with." She blew out the flame on hers and took Rog's, sliding them back in her backpack. She preferred not to leave her supplies behind. Looking around the room, she grabbed the remains of a wooden handle. "I can use it as a weapon if I have to." She shrugged her backpack into a more comfortable position and slid the wood into the straps, so she could pull it out with one hand. "It can double as a torch if needed."

Hark shrugged and handed the lit lantern to Rog and preceded to light a second one. "You never know."

"Let's go." Rog stepped in front of Grace, leading them out.

The tunnel walls were smoother here than in the mine. The bracing here a steel infrastructure, unlike the timbers in the other section.

"This doesn't make any sense." Grace hadn't seen anything like this in her lifetime. "This has to be hundreds of years old."

"It probably predates the apocalypse." Rog's voice carried a bit of awe in it.

They continued, following the tunnel. The stone floors were smooth, the walls the same. Glass inserts embedded in the walls lay dark. Grace thought they may have been lights once upon a time. She ran her hand over one, marveling at the smoothness. The sound of their footsteps didn't even echo.

Grace's breathing became labored. The longer they walked the closer the walls seemed to come. The air harder for her to bring into her lungs. She stopped, closing her eyes. Grace took a deep breath, a shiver racing down her spine. The walls were not closing in. The just appeared to go on endlessly.

"Are you okay?" Arms pulled her in. Wrapping around her, settling her head against a strong heartbeat. Rog's arms.

The chill in her veins, warmed. Her breathing settled down. The scent of male musk, and fresh air filled her lungs, calming her panic. Another hand settled on her shoulder. A second face, breath warm against her cheek, looked at her.

"Better?" Hark's concern helped settle her.

Breathing deeply, taking as much air as possible into her lungs and releasing it, Grace nodded. She imagined being snug in her bed in her soddy. The air warm and wrapped in Rog's arms. Burying her head in his chest, eyes closed, her cheeks heated. That part was new, but the thought alone relaxed and excited her.

Grace rested, Rog's arms settling her down. "I'm okay."

Grabbing the lantern from Hark, who'd evidently grabbed it from Rog earlier, Rog wrapped an arm around her waist. "Are you okay to keep going?"

"Yes." Shame wormed its way into her thoughts. "I'm sorry."

"Hey, nothing to be sorry for." Hark smiled at her. "These tunnels are creepy. Unending and it feels like there's no way out."

Oh God, he's right. Her breathing sped up. Not again. She took a deep breath, closing her eyes. Grounding herself. Rog's arm around her. The light from the lantern, seen through her eyelids, the feel of the ground beneath her feet. The touch of her clothes against her skin.

"It's okay, Grace." Rog squeezed her against his side.

"Oops, sorry." Hark ducked his head, sending Grace a charming smile.

She laughed. "Jerk."

The men joined her, the laughter breaking the tension, releasing her fears.

"Are you okay to continue? I don't know how long we'll have to go." Rog peered at Grace, looking into her eyes.

"Yes. The unending tunnels just got to me." Grace smirked at Hark who grinned back.

Rog shook his head, a smile flitting across his lips. Her eyes snagged on them. She imagined them soft, but firm. Fleshy enough to nibble and firm enough to kiss her until her mind shattered. Grace licked her lips, parched just from her imagination.

"Let's go then. Before you two devour each other in front of me." Hark smirked.

Rog growled then shook his head. Pulling Grace along and began to walk.

"Jerk." She whispered it, hiding her laughter. She hoped.

"Yup. At least we're moving again." Mouth in a grin, Hark began to whistle.

CHAPTER FOUR

Rog rolled his eyes. He'd always need his family, but Hark was closest to him. They complemented each other.

He'd been so young when the apocalypse happened, for a dragon at any rate. His dam and sire kept them safe, hibernating in the base of the volcano of their weyr. Before that, the world no longer believed in dragons and the technology made it dangerous. It made sense until the turmoil of the world seeped its way into their dreams, waking them.

He wasn't sure he wanted a mate until he'd found his. The world so different from what he remembered. But the small body, snug against his, belonged there. Every bit of him attuned to her. And evidently Hark also. It made sense. They'd always been so close.

Not that he planned on sharing her with him. Other than the changing ceremony of course, but it was good to know that she fit. He'd seen her smirks and the subtle jabs aimed at Hark. Hopefully whenever Hark found his mate, she too would be a good fit.

His dragon wanted to stop and claim Grace right there. He'd seen his brothers. Sex first and then get to know them. He wanted more. Right up front, he let Grace know he was a dragon.

His brothers were lucky they weren't killed. Ari was stabbed, but Rog knew it was Ari's fault. His own mate stabbed him. Not that she knew it. But he totally deserved it.

Rog wanted no secrets. So far, Grace handled his revelations with astonishing acceptance. He just hoped she continued.

Her panic attack, if that's what it was, turned her instinctively to him. Her arms wrapped around his waist, her breath warm against his chest, thickened his blood. Set his pulse to thumping and squeezed his heart in joy. He could ignore the other parts for now. The throbbing of his penis, and the yearning to be one. For now, it was enough she walked beside him.

Content, Rog paced himself to Grace.

Hark's whistling echoed through the tunnel.

The floor subtly angled down. Not enough to notice unless you were paying attention. He did. The lantern shed a glow around them, leaving the rest of the tunnel dark. Shifting his eyes, letting his dragon look out, Rog noticed a dull glow ahead.

We need to be on our guard. I see light ahead.

Not much.

Maybe it is from outside.

No, it's too even. It is definitely man made.

Do you think they could still be alive down here? Hark sounded doubtful, his brows tightening.

Nothing would surprise me. Humans have survived an apocalypse.

So did cockroaches. Harks dry comment loosened the tightness in his chest.

Rog chuckled. He couldn't help it.

"What's so funny?" Grace looked up at him. Her brows almost nonexistent they were so fair. "Or were you two talking in your heads again?"

"Yes, and just a comment by Hark."

Grace's eyes slid to look at Hark suspiciously, then lips pursed, moved ahead.

She obviously didn't want to know what he said.

Rog couldn't wait to get to know Grace better. He loved to tease and she would find that out, but hopefully after they were mated. She seemed to handle Hark well, and he was just as bad.

With a grin, Rog leaned over and kissed the top of Grace's head.

She looked up at him, frowning and cocking her head, slowing to look at him, her brow raised in question.

A smile still on his face, he planted a kiss on her forehead. "No reason. You make me feel happy." Rog pulled ahead, deliberately keeping Grace behind him.

Lights meant humans. The tunnel must have been barricaded centuries ago. Though Rog doubted anyone could still be alive down here, he couldn't discount it. He preferred to be ready.

Treading closer, he brought his dragon closer to the surface. He sharpened his eyesight. The flame from the lantern dimmed, the glow defining the nooks and crannies further down. Still nothing looked suspicious. The passageway bent, just past the light.

Rog motioned, waving Grace and his brother to stop. "Stay back, just a bit. There's a corner ahead. I want to look before you two go near."

Grace grumbled but stopped. Hark looked ready to argue.

Please, brother, guard my mate.

Hark bowed his head. *Fine, if that's what you want.*

Knowing Grace would be safe, Rog eased to the corner. Something bothered him. The tunnel so far wasn't unusual. Except for the fact the door locked from the outside and inside. And there was light. Man-made light. Not phosphorescent rock, which he'd expect.

Rog didn't know how many years had passed since the apocalypse, how many generations of humans since they lost most of the population. But he doubted humans would willingly have given up all they'd known. He wondered if the Blue Ridge Mountains would reveal secrets most humans didn't even know about.

Looking around the bend, he saw more of the same tunnel. Cautiously, moving forward, the air changed. His dragon acted, crouching, and hurtling him forward with a burst of speed.

Stay back! There's a trap. Positive Hark guarded Grace, Rog looked back. Spears and shards of metal embedded one side of the wall. His lips curled, nostrils flaring. Most of them wouldn't have hurt his dragon, but they would have killed Grace. Baring his teeth, a low growl emanating from his throat, Rog checked for further dangers.

Sound farther down the tunnel alerted him. Whipping around, Rog's dragon took over. His bulk filled the tunnel, preventing any passage. Stomping, going toward the noise, his growl reverberated. A hissing filled the air.

Go back! Poison!

A burst of flame erupted from his mouth. The gasses rising from the rock caught flame, exploding. The tunnel creaked, walls shifting, but nothing fell. Here. His hearing picked up falling rock, but he saw nothing.

Are you safe? Did the walls collapse by you?

We're fine. I dragged Grace back. She keeps trying to get to you.

Let her know I'm fine. If I find nothing else, you can follow.

So, there is someone there?

I don't know. There are no foot prints. The dust hasn't been disturbed for years. These could have been set up long ago. They are all passive defenses.

But obviously they are guarding something.

Yessss. I see a fork in the tunnel.

Glancing both ways, Rog realized the turn led to a door. Shifting back to his human form, Rog tried the doorknob. It was locked. Twisting it harder, he heard the mechanism break. The door swung in. A metal staircase led down, lighted by a gentle glow.

There is a door, and a staircase leads down.

We're coming.

I don't know if that's wise.

Harks snort wasn't hard to identify. *You can't stop us.*

Rog grinned, knowing Hark was eager to explore. If it wasn't for Grace, he'd be loving this. His worry over her safety, grounded him.

I'll wait here for you then.

Rog peered down the staircase. Nothing stirred. His pulse sped up. He shifted from leg to leg, waiting for them to arrive.

Grace reached him first, eyes sparkling with excitement. She hugged him. "Did you find anything?"

"Not yet."

Hark arrived on her tail, his eyes glowing. "Let's go, then."

"Give me room, just in case there are more boobytraps."

Grace grimaced, but let Rog go down first. Hopefully seeing the traps he'd sprung scared her enough to keep her listening.

His steps reverberated on the steel stairs. Each step felt on the railing. He worried they would run into another boobytrap at the bottom. It seemed a logical spot to have one. Rog could see the end of the stairs. The floor below was gray. If he had to guess, he'd say it was white, but the dust covered everything, muting any possibility of color.

"Stay here. Let me make sure there are no more boobytraps."

"Be careful." Grace placed a small hand on his arm. "Please."

Rog nodded, heart light. She cared.

Carefully stepping down, he moved away from the stairs, circling the bottom, testing for any traps. "I don't think there are any here. You can come on down."

Grace nimbly stepped down.

Hark, hard on her heals, looked around, eyes wide. "This is turning into a letdown." He took a deep breath, sighing.

Rog nodded, hands on his hips. He looked around. The room was empty. A long counter covered one wall, a sink in one end. Not even any cabinets, the counter just floated on the wall. Two doors led off the room. Both shut. One below the stairs and one opposite.

Grace frowned. "You'd think since someone took so much time to protect this area, it would be more interesting." She walked over to the counter, tapped it, glanced underneath and shook her head. "I'm surprised this lasted."

"Probably because it hasn't been used in so long." Hark looked around. "I don't think it's ever been used."

"It has." Grace reached into the sink and brought out a mug. Her nose wrinkling. "Whatever was in here is black." She poked her finger into the cup. "And solid."

"Let's keep moving. Which door do you want to try next?" The doors were opposite each other. Rog was happy to turn the decision over to Grace.

"This one." She went over to the door below the stairs.

Rog slid in front of her before she could turn the handle. "I go first."

She rolled her eyes and stepped back.

Maybe she didn't pay attention to the traps. He'd protect her even if it was from herself.

Rog turned the handle and pulled the door toward him. A soft glow lit the inside. It was a small room, filled with shelves.

Grace stuck her head beneath his arm. "Ooh, a supply room." She ducked around him, entering the room. "I wonder if there is anything useful here."

Hark snorted and turned away. "Not likely."

Rog leaned against the door, admiring Grace's figure bending and twisting. "Let her look." His pants tightened, watching her heart shaped butt wiggle while she kneeled on the ground, reaching to check out different items abandoned years ago.

She checked every item. Some crumbled in her touch. Others brought a frown to her face. A couple of items made it into the bucket. Rog wasn't sure what they were and didn't know if Grace did either. Regardless, it looked as if they were going with.

How's she doing in there? Ready to check out the rest? Hark stood with the other door open, looking past it. *Mind if I explore a bit?*

Wait. Who knows what we'll find down here? I'll see if Grace is ready to move on.

"Can we check out the other door? Not much in here." Grace asked. She grabbed the bucket, setting it down at the bottom of the stairs. "I'll grab it when we go back up."

Rog followed. "We're ready to continue." He let Hark take the lead. Grace followed and he took up the rear.

Stepping past the door, he realized they were in a corridor. Wide enough for a dragon to fly and carved from the mountain itself. The floor had been treated, making it smooth. Multiple doors led off it. Rog groaned.

***

Grace couldn't believe it. How on earth could a place this big be hidden?

Rog's groan made her belly twist. She wondered what so many rooms were needed for. They couldn't be more tunnels. None of the tunnels had doors leading to them. Hark was striding toward the first one. The slap of his feet making Grace realize he walked barefoot.

"Don't you have any shoes?" She squeezed her eyes shut, realizing how rude her question sounded. "Sorry." This is why she didn't people.

"He probably left them upstairs." Rog shrugged, obviously unconcerned.

Hark was a big boy and he didn't seem bothered by it. She shouldn't be either.

Rog urged her forward. Grace sucked in a deep breath at the warmth of his hand against her back. Ignoring the flutters in her belly, she followed Hark, quickening her steps away from Rog. She didn't quite move fast enough. His touch continued to make her ache in places she'd rather not think about.

"No, I lost them. Doesn't matter. My feet are tough." Hark pushed open a door.

Grace followed, slamming into his back. Her attention centered more on the man behind her, rather than the one in front. She didn't notice he stopped, creating a living breathing brick wall. "Sorry."

"Check this out." Sweeping his arm in front of him, Hark moved further into the room.

Grace's jaw dropped. Fascinated, she walked further in.

Behind her Rog exclaimed. "Holy shit."

She spun around the center of the room. Grace never thought to find something like this in an old abandoned mine. One abandoned long before the apocalypse.

"I want to see the other rooms." She ran to one of the doors leading from the room. A light went on when the door opened. She stopped. Other than a layer of dust, and not much of that, the room was pristine.

Grace walked over, hesitantly touching the bed. She pushed on it. It was soft. This must be a mattress. One from before. She looked back at the door, hearing just murmurs of conversation. Leaned on it, putting much of her weight on it. Standing back, she couldn't stop the grin crossing her face.

Grace clamored on top, stretching out, spreading her arms and legs. Like sitting on a cloud. Her head on the pillow, she let herself sink onto the mattress. So soft. She couldn't stop the groan spilling from her throat. She never wanted to leave this bed. The room wasn't drafty, muddy or wet.

"Are you okay?" Rog raced into the room. Stopping, he looked at her and grinned. "Enjoying yourself?"

"Um hm. I could stay here all day." Grace wiggled, turning her face to Rog. "I've never felt a mattress like this."

"You can, if you'd like." Rog strode over to the side of the bed, leaning over her. Running a finger across cheek. "I'd be happy to join you."

Heat streaked up her cheeks. She squirmed. "No, I want to see what else is down here."

Rog leaned over and kissed her forehead. "If you're sure."

His grin twisted her insides, heat blooming from deep in her abdomen. She sucked in a breath, paralyzed. No one ever kissed her like that before, looked at her like that. The wicked twinkle in his eye sent desire spiraling through her body.

No, she wasn't sure. She'd like to just grab Rog around the neck and pull him down on her. The look on his face told her he'd like nothing better. "Yes."

Stepping back, Rog grabbed her hands, pulling her off the bed. "Up and at 'em."

Grace slid, leaning against the bed and trapped once again in his arms. She looked up into his eyes and sighed.

Rog stepped back, a smirk on his face, and the devil in his eyes. "Ladies first."

Grace gulped, waving her hand to try to cool off her red cheeks. "Okay." She darted around Rog, sliding into the living room. With a wistful glance around, Grace headed into the hallway.

Hark was already opening a door across the way.

"What do you see?"

"It looks like the same, living areas with bedrooms and a bath."

Grace debated on following him, but instead took the next door down. Opening it, she looked around, admiring the kitchen and family room. Peeking into the other doors she saw bedrooms and a bath.

It was sparkling. Her curiosity dragged her further in the bath. Hesitantly looking around, she turned the faucet. Startled, she jumped back. The water rushed into the sink and down the drain. She turned it off. Looking at the toilet, Grace shrugged and hit the lever. With a whoosh, the water sucked down, replaced with more clean water.

This would make a wonderful home. Taking a deep breath, Grace wandered back into the main room.

Rog stood in the door leading to the corridor, watching her.

Ignoring him, Grace ran her hand over the counter top. Smooth and cool to the touch. The counter appeared to be stone. Quartz or granite, she didn't know which. Durable. Opening up a cabinet, her jaw dropped.

Inside were matching dishes, white and sparkling. She opened and closed the door. The cabinet appeared to have some sort of seal, keeping out dust. She went from cupboard to cupboard. They were filled, ready to use at a moment's notice.

Plates, cups, bowls, and glasses filled the cabinets. The drawers carried silverware, measuring spoons, cooking aids, more than Grace had ever seen before. Opening the last door, Grace gasped. A pantry, almost as big as the whole kitchen. On shelves, silver bags were stocked and labeled. Her father always said mylar bags were good forever, but she'd never believed him. Picking up a bag, Grace shook it. It didn't rip or tear. "Look at all this."

"What is it?" Rog straightened up, peering around the corner at the bag in her hand.

"Food. Staples, mixes, just about anything you'd need. Like for a hundred years." She couldn't keep the awe out of her voice. "Even if it has gone stale, it's more than I've seen in one place in my life. It's hard to get enough flour to make bread. Harvesting the wheat, grinding it, takes months."

Grace placed the bag on the shelf, putting it exactly back where she got it from. "I can see why whoever put this here locked it up. I just don't understand why they never came back."

"Maybe they weren't finished. It could be the apocalypse hit and they never made it back."

"Maybe." Grace looked at all the food. "What if it's all still good?" A grin crossed her face. "That would be awesome."

"Let's check out the rest of the facility. See what else we can find." Rog's arm circled her waist, gently pulling her away. Shutting the door to the pantry, he released her.

Excitement zapped through her veins. This time it wasn't because of Rog's touch. Well, not all of it. Grace loved to explore. Without Rog and his brother to open the door, she might never have discovered this place. She'd tried the locks to no avail. Since they were now open, she needed to see it all.

"This is so awesome." Throwing a hug around his neck, she squeezed tight and released him. Having someone to share it with made it even more so. "Let's check it all out."

Grace headed back out into the corridor. Rog followed behind her, his presence turning her insides warm. A sense of safety surrounded her, because of him.

Hark was further down, opening another door.

"What have you found?" Rog's voice sent shivers down her spine.

"Everything's the same. Living area, bedrooms and bathrooms." Hark hollered back.

"Did everyone have a pantry?" Grace asked.

Hark stopped, turned and looked at her, frowning. "I never opened anything. Just looked at the layouts."

Grace frowned. Maybe they lived as dragons and didn't care about comfort. The pantry probably didn't hold much interest when a meal to them was a cow or two each. "Well, I want to check."

"How about we find out how many units there are, then we check." Rog cajoled.

"I want to see if they all hold that much food." It was important to her. That much food, the variety could feed her family for a long time. Even if they didn't want to move here, the food could be brought to them. "It would be easy to check. I'd just have to open the pantry door."

"Food? What food?" Hark perked up.

"I'll show you." Grace, seizing on Hark's interest, darted into the nearest room.

He followed, butting in ahead of Rog. "Where?"

Grace opened the door in the kitchen. It looked like part of the cabinets, so she hadn't noticed until she opened it up. "Right here." She waved at all the bags lining the shelves.

"That's food?" Hark didn't look impressed.

Come to think of it, neither had Rog. Maybe they didn't have to worry about rationing in the cold months. Grace couldn't remember a winter that hadn't been lean. "Those are storage bags filled with food." She pointed. "Look. Flour, sugar, brown sugar, egg noodles, rice. Everything you'd need to cook with and some I've never heard of."

"There is a place like this in each unit. Filled with silver bags. I just didn't know what it was." He shrugged. "I didn't bother to read the labels."

"Every one?" Grace couldn't imagine the amount of food stored. Even if some of it was bad, it was a huge amount. "That's amazing."

"How many have you found so far?" Rog asked.

"Including the first one, I counted ten units so far. All the same." Hark appeared to be adding in his head, judging by each bob of his head along with his fingers flicking out.

"Let's assume all of them are tricked out the same. Let's peek in each door to check and see how many we find. We can always explore each one more later." Rog looked askance at Grace.

"Sounds good to me." Hark left, his large body moving quicker than Grace thought would be possible. "I'll take the right side."

Grace laughed. "I guess we'll take the left side." Running out, she saw Hark sticking his head in doors, slamming them and going to the next. Opening the next, she saw a repeat living area and closed the door. Determined to find out how many there were, Grace ran to the next. She'd catch up to Hark, yet.

A few doors down, her face heated. She turned to Rog. "Can you count them while I check?" She looked, saw Hark further away. Her competitive streak urging her on.

"I already was." Rog's laughter reignited the flame in her belly.

Her heartbeat drummed in her ears. The joy she felt, the task ahead of her and hope for her future filled her. Hugging Rog, she raced off, whooping down the corridor.

CHAPTER FIVE

Rog smiled, his steps light. He followed Grace, keeping a mental tab of units. His gaze caressing her figure. His hands couldn't yet, as much as he wanted to. Her skittishness warned him of that. Grace spent too much time alone. Unused to other people.

Perhaps it wasn't the fact she spent too much time alone, but she didn't know how to respond to him. She'd mentioned her family but no one else. He'd seen the beautiful flush creeping over her face at his touch.

A sly grin touched his face. He'd just have to touch her more. Get closer to her. Maybe his goal of bonding to her was closer than he imagined. He couldn't just fling her over his shoulder and ravish her, but caressing her?

Rog's heart beat faster, his groin tightening. Gentling her? Oh, he could picture it. Groaning softly, Rog walked faster. He wasn't about to let Grace leave his sight.

Hark and Grace were racing down the corridor. Their laughter echoing down the uninhabitable corridor. Slamming doors, pounding feet, gave life to an otherwise deserted tomb. Rog hoped it would remain that way.

The passage way finally turned.

"Wait for me." Rog hollered, his voice carrying easily.

Hark stopped, grabbed Grace around the neck and rubbed his nose in her hair.

Grace shoved him away, or tried to. When he didn't stop, she kicked him in the shin.

"Oww. Mean girl." Hark grinned, stepping back.

Grace stuck her tongue out, laughing at him.

Rog shook his head, a smile on his face. "I counted fifty rooms. How about you?" He questioned his brother.

"Same."

Room for a hundred families, buried in the mountain, unused.

"It just doesn't make sense. Why would no one have come back? And why was the door locked from the outside and inside. How could it have been done?" Grace grimaced.

"Maybe we'll find answers down here." Hark walked around the corner. "This is not quite as long as the last tunnel."

Grace rolled her eyes.

Rog stifled his laugh, placed a hand at her waist and moved toward his brother. Turning the corner, his shoulders dropped. The lengthy passage stretched out before them. Doors lined on one side rather than two, but it would still take longer than he wanted to complete.

If this was the only one. Rog has his doubts. This hidden compound reminded him of a dragon weyr. It's twists and turns found whenever you'd least expect it.

"Oh man, check this out." Hark stuck his head out of a doorway. "Take a look at this."

They crowded through the door. Stepping inside Rog became speechless.

"Wow." Grace darted in further. Row upon row of plastic piping filled the room. Dead stalks on the ground while others bloomed. The sound and scent of water moving through the pipes. "What is a hydroponics room?" She pointed to a peeling sign on the wall.

"Evidently this is." Hark smirked, reading the door, tapping his finger on the words there.

"Funny." Grace tossed her head.

"I'd assume it is growing plants in water." Rog poked his finger in a pipe that lay open. In all the pipes, there were spots evidently for plants. Some had wild growth and others were jammed full of dead stalks and leaves. The floor here littered with old rotting growth.

"Well, let's see what the other rooms are." Grace headed out the door first, skipping down the hall to the next door.

Rog grabbed her hand. "Please wait for me. We don't know that every room will be empty." He felt the shiver through her arm. She held on, slanting a shy smile at him. His heart bloomed. He was growing on her.

Head held high, Rog led them to the next door. It had agriculture written on the door. Looking at each other, they shrugged. He had no clue what that would encompass. Sliding in front of Grace, Rog opened the door and entered, ensuring there were no traps.

"Wow." Hark stood there looking around. "Bet everything in here needs power of some sort."

"Yeah." Grace looked around her eyes wide. "Maybe." She started circling the room.

Rog recognized some of the equipment. Before the world became so reliant on technology, humans used other means to grow food. He hadn't spent much time in the human world before, but enough to recognize some things. "There is equipment here that can be used. If it hasn't seized up from non-use."

He heard a squeal. His guess, a happy one.

"What's wrong?" Hark looked around, frowning. Trying to find Grace.

"That's a happy noise. She made it when she found the silver bags of food." Rog started trotting in the direction it had come from. Just in case he was wrong. He rounded a corner and found Grace looking through shelves lining a wall.

She turned, ran up to Rog and threw her arms around his neck. She squeezed, still squealing.

Wrapping his arms around her, Rog hugged her to him. Her curves, hidden under her clothes pressed against him. His hand made contact with her warm, silky skin. He slid it inside, around her waist, spreading his fingers. On the curve of her buttock and up her back. Rog hardened against her, his cock aching.

"Oh." Her breathing exclamation against his neck sent a shudder through his body.

He pulled her tighter. "What has you so excited?" He couldn't help the roughness in his voice. It was all he could do to push words out his throat.

"Seeds." She wiggled in his arms, trying to get away.

Pressing her hips against him, loving the ache she brought him to, he couldn't help but nibble on her tempting earlobe.

Her shiver sent his lips skating down her neck. So soft, he wanted to gobble her up.

"You two could go back to one of the bedrooms. I'm willing to check out the rest of the place myself." Hark's snicker making Grace freeze under Rog's hands.

Grace's neck heated. "No."

Rog peeked. A blush slid up and over her cheeks. He bet it covered her body. He wanted to find out. But her wiggles to free herself were in earnest now. Rog loosened his arms, letting Grace slide down his body. Agony, but worth every throb in his veins. He released her.

Peeking up at him from beneath her lashes, her cheeks aflame, Grace caressed his jaw. "I want to continue."

Rog shrugged. He knew she would. It was important his mate was happy. This exploration, the things they were finding, thrilled her. Rog hoped if the items were no longer good, Grace wouldn't be too disappointed. "I thought so."

"I'm going to need food soon." Hark rubbed his stomach. "I'm surprised you didn't think a beast was down here."

Grace snickered. "I'm sure I knew I was down here with two."

Rog laughed. "We could go back and eat."

"After all, I did catch two buffalo." He turned toward the entrance. "And we can come back down."

"I hope you didn't harm the skin. I can make a coat from it. It will help keep the cold away in winter."

"I can help keep the cold away in winter." Rog couldn't help but whisper in her ear.

Her tinted cheeks were his reward.

"I'm hungry too." His growl couldn't be helped. His hunger for Grace was growing. He'd thought his brothers moved too fast with their mates, but he understood now. How he was going to stop from grabbing her and tossing her on the nearest bed, he didn't know.

"Let's eat then." Grace skittered away from him. Heading out the door and back the way they came.

They passed the corner and Grace broke away, darting into the first room they'd found.

Rog poked his head in.

Grace grabbed a couple of silver bags and then pulled a skillet from the cupboards. She turned around, sliding to a stop. She lifted the bag. "I wanted to try these. See if they're still good."

Her grin, the happiness showing in her eyes lifted Rog's heart. As much as he wanted to bury himself in her, the joy she exuded brightened his life. Regardless of how he touched her, just knowing she now was part of his life brought him immeasurable bliss.

***

Rog's looks sent heat flashing through her. The man lit her body on fire. One glance, whoosh, flames shot through her. Her rock-hard nipples hurt, begging for his touch. Her core ached, liquid and wanting. It scared her.

He called up reactions she'd never experienced before. Plus, he was a dragon. An animal. Smoothing down her top, she swallowed. He made her feel like an animal.

Biting her lip, she snuck a look at Rog. Her cheeks flooded with heat.

He was looking at her.

Her belly churned, seeing the lust on his face. So far, he hadn't forced his attentions on her. Her chest tightened. But she was pretty sure she wanted him to.

Grace skidded around him. Her voice strangled. She couldn't get another word out if she tried. Not wanting just meat, though the thought of roasted buffalo had her mouth watering, Grace grabbed a package of vegetables and biscuit mix.

Hopefully, no animal smelled the kill and wandered in the mine shaft. She didn't know if just the men's presence, since they could shift into dragons, would deter any predators. She hoped so.

The empty rooms, while filled with amazing things from the past, creeped Grace out just a bit. She kept looking over her shoulder for ghosts. She wondered if they would ever know what happened to the people who had prepared this shelter for their future needs. If they knew their futures would never come.

Going through the door to the stairs, Grace saw Hark already grabbed the bucket she'd set there. It would be good for water and carrying food. Not so good to use in the fire to cook. Grace bounced up the stairs, thinking of all the pots and pans in the living quarters. If this one held up to the fire, hopefully the rest would also.

Hark stayed in the lead.

Rog pulled her back. They were nearing where the gasses ignited earlier.

Hark stepped through the section, giving a thumbs up when he safely crossed.

Rog's hands on her shoulders were distracting her. Her attention centering more on the warmth seeping from them than on the possible traps.

"The knives and spears are still in the wall. Shouldn't that trap be fine?" Grace looked at them, embedded in the wall.

"Better safe than sorry. Hark's hide is tough. If he gets another little prick, he'll be okay."

"Funny." Hark rolled his eyes. "Better than being a prick." Hark turned his head, baring his fangs at Rog.

Grace let out a long breath. Dragons or men, they behaved exactly like her brothers.

Soon enough, they were back out the door and in the mine. Grace hunched her shoulders, walking back to the fire. It seemed so much colder and dirtier here. The contrast between the hidden rooms below and the mine up here seemed like night and day. Even though the mountain was the same.

One buffalo lay partially blocking the entrance. She assumed the other was behind it or on the ledge outside the mine. Shaking her head, ignoring the banter between the brothers going on behind her, Grace grabbed her knife from her sheath. It was time to skin it. Knowing the men behind her could eat the animal whole, she really wanted the pelt before they dug in.

Standing over it, she realized it wasn't going to be easy. Larger than the cattle and deer she normally dressed, it also weighed more. Pushing on its side got her nowhere. Standing straight, Grace looked at the animal. Looking up at the roof of the mine, no hook magically appeared. She turned her head, eyeing up the brothers. They could become dragons. She'd bet it wouldn't be any issue for them to hold the carcass up so she could skin them.

"Could you two lend me a hand?" Grace watched Rog turn eagerly toward her.

"What do you need?" Rog strode over, Hark on his heels.

"I need the buffalo strung up, but there is no place to do it." She glanced down, then back up, looking into Rog's eyes. "Do you think your dragons are strong enough to hold them up while I skin them?"

"Of course." Rog puffed up before her eyes, strutting over to look at the buffalo.

Grace could barely contain a giggle.

"Whoa. Just wait a minute. You want our dragons to hold up the buffalo while you are in front of us, wielding a knife?" Hark looked at Rog. "She could just as easily gut us as the animal."

Rog frowned, scowling at his brother. "I trust her."

Grace preened, then realized she looked like Rog a few minutes ago. "I wouldn't. I want a buffalo pelt more than I want scales to keep me warm."

Hark laughed. "Hear that, Rog? You're out of luck."

Her cheeks bloomed with fire. Grace ducked her head, not looking either one in the eye.

Rog growled, advancing on his brother.

If they fought, and it looked like they might, the buffalo could be destroyed. Grace grabbed Rog's arm. "Wait. Half an hour tops and I'll be done. Please."

Hark grinned, dancing toward the mine entrance.

Rog glared, but didn't move. "Fine. Stand back. I need to shift."

Grace moved toward the side, giving him room. Her eyes widened.

Rog stripped his clothes off, stretching when he was done. Then suddenly a dragon stood in his place.

Grace swallowed. Her throat suddenly dry. Maybe she should be the one worried.

The dragon watched her. His gold eyes gleamed. His tail twitched, swishing back and forth.

Hesitantly she stepped forward, hand out.

Rog, she could tell it was him, even in this form, rubbed his head against her. Nudging her closer, until she stood against him.

Her hand touched his scales. Grace sucked in a breath. They were warm to the touch. Softer than she'd thought. They reminded her of hard leather.

Rog nudged her again, pushing her away. He twisted and picked up the buffalo. By one leg.

Grace laughed. "No, you have to hold both legs. Both rear legs."

Rog cocked his head, gave her a toothy grin and grabbed both legs, swinging it in front of her.

She could read the mischief on his face. Grabbing the front leg, Grace stopped it. "Now lower it, please."

Rog dropped it down so the front feet rested on the floor. Jiggling it so it looked like it was dancing.

Shaking her head, she couldn't keep the grin off her face. "Oh, you're nothing but trouble, aren't you?"

The dragon snorted, echoed by one behind her.

"You pegged him. Trouble." Hark laughed. "When will you need me to hold the other?"

"Once the skin is off, and I'll gut it and carve a couple of flank steaks for me and I'll be ready for the second one." She patted the dragon's leg. "Then it's all yours."

"Great. I'll change when you get to that point, so you can start on the second one."

"Thank you."

"Just don't get me with the knife." Hark flicked her nose and headed outside.

Grace cut a slit down the stomach, then around each knee joint. She then slit from the center cut up each limb to the knee. She sliced around the neck. Grace figured she could strip the head later. From the rumbles emanating from the belly of the dragon, he needed food. Better the buffalo than her.

Quickly fleshing the skin from the body, Grace stripped the skin off. Hopefully she didn't waste any meat, leaving any on the skin. It would just make it harder to tan later. "I wish I had some salt to keep them moist."

"Maybe there is some below in the tunnels." Hark answered.

"Oh, I can store them in that first room, too." Grace jumped up, running over to hug Hark. "What a great idea."

"Won't that stink?" Hark wrinkled his nose.

Grace heard a growl and flinched. She looked back at the dragon. His glare let her know he didn't appreciate her hugging Hark. She headed back to him, rubbing his snout. "Knock it off. He just gave me an idea. I don't have the time or supplies to tan the hides right now, but Hark mentioned I might be able to use supplies from below."

She went back to the buffalo. Making a couple of precision cuts, the guts tilted out. Grace made a few slices and pulled out a couple of steaks. "There. You can have the rest." She stepped back, grabbing the steaks. She placed the steaks in the cast iron frying pan she'd brought up. She tried to pick up the hide. The heavy fur made it harder to maneuver than she thought it would be. She tugged it, heaving it behind her. Barely managing to drag it to the side of the cave.

A crunch sent her head peering over her shoulder. The dragon, Rog, munched on the remains of the buffalo. Turning toward the entrance, Grace saw another dragon. Dark scaled like Rog, Hark's scales gleamed in the weak sunlight.

He lifted the animal, keeping it within her reach.

"Thank you."

Hark snorted, preening.

A grunt answered him back from Rog, followed by another crunch.

Grace repeated her movements, efficiently slicing the skin and fur off. Diving in, she grabbed the flank steaks from this one too and stepped back. The steaks slid in her hands. She moved to juggle to keep them from falling.

"I'm done. Thank you."

Grabbing the pelt, she dragged it behind her, grunting. Or tried. She swore this one was even heavier. Hark was right. It did smell. "When you're done, can you move the skin and put it with the other one?" It was too hard to do by herself. She'd have to get one of the men to assist her in salting the skin.

Crunching filled the cavern. Grabbing one of the mylar containers, Grace opened it. Inside was multiple sealed bags. Grace beamed. Humming she dumped out the bags. Taking three of the steaks, she used the big bag to place them in it.

That should keep them from getting dirty. She hadn't brought anything other than hardtack and trail mix. The steaks were bonus. The buffalo skins were a huge bounty.

Reading a bag, Grace followed directions. She added water to the skillet, then added the contents. Green beans. Her tummy growled. Adding an old grate on top of the fire, Grace laid out a steak.

Grabbing the second large silver bag, she opened it. It, too, had smaller bags inside. Excitement bubbled inside her. Biscuits. Not hardtack. No, Bisquick it said. But regardless it was made from honest to God flour. Using the bag as a mixing bowl, she followed directions and soon had little balls of goodness ready to cook. Setting them on the grate next to the steak, Grace's stomach fluttered. She so hoped they were still good. She leaned in, sniffing the air. Enjoying the scent of sizzling meat and baking bread.

Checking the frying pan, the beans were plumped up and green. She thought about the butter and spices in her soddy, wishing they were here. Rubbing her hands together, a smile she couldn't keep off her face, Grace watched her food.

Twisting to check on the dragons, a crinkle by her feet had her leaning over. Grace grabbed the bags on the floor and combined the contents into one large bag. She counted the number of bags, smiling with glee. She placed it against the wall, next to her hides and along with the bag holding her steak. She couldn't help but dance a little jig. Winter would be so much easier to survive now.

A hand touched her shoulder.

Grace screamed and flipped around. She sagged against the side of the mine, heart racing. Intent on her food, she stopped paying attention to her surroundings. She'd missed Rog and Hark shifting back.

Both of them stood in front of her grinning.

Jerks.

CHAPTER SIX

Watching Grace do a little dance of happiness made his heart swell. She focused intently on her food. So much that he could hear her heart racing after he tried to get her attention.

He tried but couldn't suppress his amusement. Her glare tickled his funny bone. The only other person he knew who concentrated that much over food was his brother Crag.

"Sorry. I didn't realize you didn't hear us." Rog felt the need to apologize, but obviously Grace didn't buy it.

Her tapping toes and narrowed eyes proved that.

"Your food smells done." Hark stared at the fire. "It smells good."

Grace rushed over. Grabbing a plate from her backpack, she loaded the steak, a couple of white things and beans onto it. "You can help yourself to the rest."

Hark, of course, went to grab it all.

"Save some for me." He dropped the buffalo hide against the wall, on top of the other one. Rog wanted to try what had Grace all excited. He hoped for her sake it tasted good. The weird silver bags meant something to her other than food. She must think they preserved food longer. She was willing to eat them to find out. So, he would too.

Hark ate anything and everything. Even if they were no longer good, he'd still eat it.

Rog wrinkled his nose and popped a white thing in his mouth. He hummed in appreciation. Bread. He'd always loved bread.

He glanced at Grace. She sat next to the fire, cutting up her steak. Popping a piece in her mouth she moaned. Immediately he imagined her moaning for a totally different reason. Shaking his head to clear it, though it did nothing for the ache in his pants, he watched Grace pop the bread into her mouth.

A look of astonishment filled her face. "This is wonderful." She shoved another in her mouth chewing and swallowing. "So good." She wiped the next in her steak juice, groaning when it hit her tongue.

She quickly cleaned her plate, thank god.

The throbbing in his pants with each grunt and moan had him ready to toss Grace to the ground and pound away at her.

She had no idea of what she was doing to him.

Maybe fresh air would help. He stood, walking out the entrance to look around. The rain finally stopped and weak sunlight filtered through the clouds. Not helping. Glancing over his shoulder, Grace was occupied once again with the food supplies. Stepping to the side of the opening, Rog pulled his cock out of his pants.

He hissed at the touch of his hand against his hardened flesh. Glancing back, making sure he wasn't in view, Rog grasped it firmly. Sliding his hand up and down his rigid flesh, he hissed. Tighter, faster. He thought about Grace, her silky hair and pillowy, pink lips. Faster, tighter, and he spilled in seconds. Shooting his load, he groaned.

He only hoped he'd last longer with Grace.

Enjoying yourself? Hark's amusement was evident in his voice.

Dick.

Nope, that's what you're holding. Grace heard you groaning. I persuaded her to stay here.

Crap.

Rog could hear Hark's laughter from here.

"Rog, did you need any help? What are you doing?" Grace's voice was getting louder.

His brother sounded like a hyena rather than a dragon. Asshole.

"No, I just needed some air. I'll be right back in." Rog slipped himself back in, putting himself back together. The thought of Grace seeing him with his pants down, for such a reason, was a bit ignoble.

Like he couldn't control himself. He could. He just needed a bit of relief now and then. He didn't think Grace would look at it like that. She seemed to be surrounded by an air of innocence. Whether it was true or not, he would take her at face value.

Dragon's fated mates held the dragon's heart in their hands. From what he'd observed from his brothers, their mates couldn't keep their hands of them. Grace didn't appear to have a problem doing so.

Rog knew Grace was his fated mate. His dam correctly predicted they wouldn't have an issue identifying their mate. It seemed bizarre until you met your one. Now, he'd never give her up.

Looking over the mountains, he wondered where Grace lived. From here there didn't appear to be any habitation. "Grace, where do you live?"

She popped out of the entrance. Pointing down the mountain, near the river they fished, she answered. "There. If you look about a hundred feet from the river, you can see a slight hill and a dark spot in front of it. That's my soddy."

He nodded, it blended well into the landscape. Rog wrapped his arms around her waist, her face becoming a subtle pink. He grinned in triumph, pulse pounding.

She stayed, surrounded by him, snuggling back to lean against his chest.

He trembled, or perhaps it was Grace. The heat generated between them overwhelming. He breathed in her body's bouquet. Fire and a woman's musk. His dragon's favorite scents. Her dark hair blew in the breeze, blending with his. His prick hard against the top of her buttocks and the small of her back. Aching once again.

Tightening his arms, he realized her hair and his, tangled together, would be a perfect match. Her brown eyes, rivaling the deepest bourbon let him see clear to her soul. Scrappy, she completed him perfectly.

Nibbling on her lip, she stared out over the mountains and valley below. Her lip plumped under the abuse.

Holding her, she hadn't run. Not even when it became obvious, she aroused him. Moving one hand, he grasped her jawline. Turned her face toward him.

Staring, drowning in her eyes. He lowered his face, lips resting against hers. His body caught fire. Desire rippled through him.

Grace gasped, opening her mouth. Turning her body to face him.

His tongue plunged in, licking, rubbing hers. Her nipples hard against his chest, Rog slipped a hand to grasp the weight of one. Kneading it, loving her moans. Their bodies rocked together, desperate for fulfillment.

He wanted to get to know her, have her know him. The conflagration burning through his veins couldn't be stopped. Unless Grace uttered one word.

His honor would demand it. Dragons were nothing if not honorable. Sneaky, vengeful, playful and honorable. It would suck.

"More." Grace moaned, head back while he suckled her neck.

Thank god.

"Grace! Grace are you here?" A male voice reverberated through the mountains.

Rog groaned. He slid his hand from her breast back to her waist, spreading his fingers to cover her ass. His pulse pounded in his ears. He took a deep breath, then let it out. "Someone you know?"

"What?" Grace snuggled his chest, arms wrapped around his middle.

"Grace? Where are you?" The voice was closer. Rocks skittering down the mountain told its own story. Someone was coming. From the noise, Rog would guess two someone's. Whether Grace answered or not, they knew she was here. Or guessed she would be.

Cockblockers coming! Make sure you're dressed. Rog grumbled.

Hark was probably laughing his ass off.

And make sure they can't see the door we opened. I don't know if Grace wants anyone to know what we found. Rog stared at the point the noises were coming from.

I'll block it. I don't want to share until we've checked it all out ourselves. I'll hide the bags Grace brought up too.

Good idea. Rog knew he could count on Hark. Neither of them was as reckless as their family thought, but sometimes things didn't go according to plan.

They weren't as overbearing as their brothers either, preferring a more relaxed life. Ari and Crag planned a weyr, set it up and were even now settling the baby dragons they'd adopted. Rog always assumed at some point he'd either set one up or move in with Ari and his mate.

Looking down at Grace, his heart melting, his insides gooey, he knew he would do whatever she wanted. If it was a soddy, Rog shuddered, he'd make do.

Rocks rolled beneath feet. Heavy breathing and a muttered conversation he ignored. Whoever wanted to see Grace, would have to deal with him. Two heads appeared over the ledge. Arms struggled to pull themselves up. Finally, the pair clambered over the edge, shaking their clothing and wiping their hands on their pants.

Eyes narrowed; Rog watched. Keeping his arms around Grace.

"Grace!" The man stopped, looking up. His mouth dropped, seeing Grace wrapped in his arms. "Grace, who the hell is this?"

The woman next to him frowned. Whispered one word. "Harlot."

The man turned on her. "Shut up." He strode over, blustering. "What is the meaning of this?"

Grace looked up, smirked and turned to the man. "It's a hug." Grace stayed tucked into his arm, standing beside him.

Rog slid his arm to encompass her shoulder, hugging her to his side. His dragon rumbled, not happy with the interruption of what he assumed was going to be his consummation with his mate.

"Funny." The man scratched his neck. "Do you have a fire going? I'm cold after that climb."

Grace rolled her eyes and answered. "Yes, of course."

Her hand slid into his. His heart turned over. Grace affected him like no one else. Puffing his chest out, taking a deep breath, Rog twined his fingers with hers.

"No wonder you keep sneaking off." The woman's spite had Grace lifting her nose.

The man with her spit on the ground. "Keep your mouth shut. No one wanted you here."

"Who are you people?" Rog ignored the squeeze from Grace's hand. He couldn't read her mind so didn't know if she warned him off asking or signified her approval. Chuckling to himself, he decided it was approval.

"I'm her brother, Paul." He nodded at the woman with him. "The witch is no one important."

"I'm here to make sure I'm not her future sister in law. I'm wanted to prove her behavior isn't impeccable." She snorted. "Obviously it's a good thing I came."

Grace growled. "I agree with that, Lavinia." Grace spit out her name like a dirty word. "I wouldn't marry into your family with a golden hog being offered."

Paul grimaced. "Dad thought it was time you were married. That one's brother has been petitioning him. Dad finally said he could approach you. But only if you were willing."

"Well, I'm not."

"That's why I came to warn you. I think he's going to force the issue. I'm pretty sure he found your house."

"Over my dead body." Rog tensed, heat filling his body. Grace was his. He'd flambé the man who tried to hurt her.

Paul grinned. "I'll keep my shovel handy. Just say the word."

"You know I have a house?"

Paul lifted a brow and rolled his eyes. "I do. Pretty sure the whole family does."

"You people are despicable." Lavinia marched into the mine like she owned it.

"I hate that woman." Paul snarled. "All she did was complain the whole way here. And it's not like I invited her either." He turned to Grace. "If you found anything here that is of any use, hide it."

Rog's opinion changed with every word out of Paul's mouth. Maybe Grace's family had a reason for letting her live by herself. If their neighbors were all like this Lavinia, he wouldn't want to live there either.

You could have warned me. Hark's complained. *Who is this harridan?*

A neighbor of Grace's. Probably why she lives so far from their family.

So, no one would mind if I ate her?

Rog chuckled. "We better go save my brother. He's threatening to eat that woman."

Grace snickered, then sobered. "Oh no, I don't want her to see what we found."

"I told my brother to hide everything. I had him block the tunnel also. I didn't know who was coming. Plus, it may not be safe."

"Then we should let her in there."

Rog laughed. "You really don't like her."

"No. She made my life hell, always picking on me. No one other than Paul would even stand up for me." She sighed. "But I didn't always tell my family what was happening. Most of my siblings are older than me. I was a bit unexpected."

"Unexpected?" Paul shook his head, a smile on his face. "You're young enough to be any of our children. You were a shock." He laughed. "To all of us. You brought the fact that mom and dad had sex right to the forefront." He gagged. "No one wanted that."

Grace snorted. "Grow up."

They'd reached the fire. Lavinia's sour face and Hark's posture left little doubt they didn't get along even upon such short acquaintance.

Good thing she's not my mate or I'd have to… I don't know, but something heinous.

That bad? Rog kept his amusement in. If she already pissed off Hark, the easiest going of the brothers, Lavinia needed to go.

Worse! What a bitch.

We'll get rid of her soon. I hope.

Grace slid out from under his arm.

A sense of loss hit me, even though she was right there, settling down by the fire.

"So why are you here?" Rog looked from Paul to Lavinia, crossing his arms and staring down at them.

"I wanted to warn Grace about" he jerked his head at Lavinia, "that one's brother. He's too lazy to climb all the way up here. But he might hide in her house." He glanced at Grace. "Or other places she might be at."

"My brother has a right to marry her. She should be thankful he wants her. Of course, I'll have to let him know what's going on here. That will ensure he won't. She'll be lucky if anyone wants her." Satisfaction oozed from her voice. "She might even be exiled."

Frowning, Rog asked, "Why would being exiled be an issue?"

***

That bitch. As if being exiled from the snooty people in the village would be a hardship. Grace already lived apart from them. Happily. Not to mention, and her heart raced at the realization, she now had Rog.

He wasn't acting like this was temporary. His protectiveness thrilled her. He stood there, arms crossed, glaring at Grace's brother and Lavinia. Staking claim. Joy bubbled inside her.

They could exile her all they wanted. Lavinia's family acted like their shit didn't stink. Grace's family didn't stand up to them, but they didn't let her tell them what to do either. Even though Lavinia tried. It was worse when Lavinia was one of the teachers in town. She make Grace's life hell.

"You came just to warn me about Walter?" Grace smiled, then dropped it. Paul came but he also brought Lavinia.

"And I wanted to stretch my legs. Thought I'd have some peace by myself, but that one wouldn't go home." Paul glared at Lavinia.

Paul lost his wife last year. Grace didn't know whether to give him her sympathy or congratulations. Mary had been a sweetheart, but let Lavinia, a longtime friend of hers, influence her too much. She'd turned into a harridan the last few years. She swore relief flashed in Paul's eyes at the funeral. Since then, he'd been more subdued. That would be natural now, though, having to raise his children by himself.

Lavinia sniffed. Her glare touching on everyone around the fire.

Grace's jaw tightened. She pressed her lips together to prevent words from falling out that didn't really need to be said. They might be satisfying, but she refused to let Lavinia know she bothered her.

"I'll keep Grace safe." Rog's curt answer turned her to goo.

"I'll help." Hark echoed.

Grace couldn't stop the grin stretching across her face. The sense of safety and belonging were something she really wasn't used to. Rog made her feel wanted. Her parents were too old and tired to pay much attention to Grace. All her brothers were older than her and out of the house. They really didn't have time for her, except for Paul.

Paul had been the only one to pay attention her. Perhaps because his daughter and Grace were only a few months apart and fast friends. Until Mary started pulling Lucy away, listening to others say Grace was a bad influence.

She sighed. Grace missed her friendship. But she didn't miss living in town. She didn't miss the constant harping of how a lady should behave.

Grace thought of the tunnel they found. The food preserved. Some probably went bad, but she hoped the majority was still good. None of them had any idea of when the tunnel was built. For all they knew, the facility was recent. Or perhaps they could store things longer with the technology they had before the apocalypse.

She didn't know, but hoped the mystery could be solved. The answers lingered in the tunnels. Grace was sure of it. Now she just needed to get rid of Lavinia.

"Good." Paul smiled, reaching a hand out to Rog. "Grace needs someone who cares about her in her life."

Lavinia snorted. Again.

Grace figured Lavinia lost so much of her brain through her nose, air just pinged inside her head. Or it just plain twisted in there. She was so mean. Her whole family acted like they were better than anyone else in town. Her brother, Walter, gave Grace the creeps. She shuddered thinking of him even touching her.

Rog shook Paul's hand then clapped him on the shoulder. "She'll never have to worry again."

Grace melted. Then rolled her eyes. She'd proven she could take care of herself. But it would be nice to have someone to lean on. Or even just talk to.

Her eyes lingered on Rog's tall form. His midnight black hair barely reaching his shoulders. His gleaming golden eyes lit a fire within her. His lips, Grace drew in a deep breath, turned her body into putty. His strong form, rough hands and more importantly, the goodness in his soul drew her to him. She needed to touch him. Prove he was real.

Grace moved, coming up from behind him, wrapping her arms around him. Closing her eyes, feeling the heat Rog generated, and a smile tipped her lips.

Rog's hand covered her arms, pulling her tighter against him.

She hoped he planned on staying. Grace surely needed him in her life. With a sigh she released him.

"Well, I should get back. It will take until night to get home." Blowing out a gust of air, Paul glanced at Lavinia. "I originally planned to stay, but…"

"I understand. I don't want her here either." Grace hugged Paul. Whispering in his ear, "come back without her. I want to show you what we found."

"I'll see you, later. Maybe next week." Paul winked letting her know he heard her. Stepping back, he nodded toward Lavinia. "I don't want to be stuck with this one in my life. It's time to go."

"Stay safe on the way home." Grace hugged Paul again. "Don't let this one drive you to murder."

"I never. Believe me, this idea of my brother marrying you is dead. I'll make sure of it."

Paul grinned. "Good. I'll hold you to that." He took the first step of the path leading down.

"Take my arm, help me down the mountain." Lavinia's grating voice echoed.

"Nope. I didn't ask you to come. I told you not to come." Paul's voice coming further along the trail.

Grace knew he was making good time. She could hear Lavinia scrabbling after him. She stifled a chuckle. They were too close still and Grace didn't want her deciding to stay.

"It was my duty to my brother." Lavinia's screech made her ears ache.

"Screw your brother. You're just a nosey old biddy." Paul tossed back.

"I'm not old! I'm years younger than you, you, you… beast." Lavinia's volume increased.

"Then you should be able to climb down by yourself."

Lavinia's scream of frustration sent Grace, Rog and Hark to chuckling.

"I don't like that woman." Hark grinned. "Maybe a dragon should grab her and dump her miles from here."

"Tempting." Grace laughed. "But the whole town is like her. Well, most of them." She then sighed. "That's the main reason I'm out here. Living near the cattle and making a life for myself. It was better being alone than living there."

Rog grabbed her up in his strong, warm arms. "You'll never be alone again."

Grace wrapped her arms around him, burying her face against his neck. "Good."

"Do you two want to do more exploring? I know it's getting late. Or do you want to just leave it for tomorrow?" Hark shrugged. "Either is fine with me."

Rog nuzzled her ear, sending shivers straight to her nipples. "What do you want to do?"

Grace moaned. "I'd like to explore, but if they turn back for some reason, I don't want Lavinia to see what we found."

Rog nodded. His face warm against hers. No one ever really listened to her before or asked her opinion. That they would and did what she wanted was indescribable. Elation filled her heart.

They could spend the night below, in one of the living areas they discovered. The thought of sharing a bed with Rog sent her body into a meltdown, but until they knew more about why no one was there, it was safer to stay up here. What if gas permeated the area, killing all of them? If they were murdered in their beds? If…

She shook her head. Ridiculous. They'd found no bodies. No evidence of anyone living there. Only new, unused areas. Sealed food and dead plants. Rooms full of items to use that hadn't been.

"What are you thinking?" Rog peered down at her. His golden eyes questioning.

"That until we know why no one is below, it would be safer to spend the night here."

Both Rog and Hark groaned. The iron rod in Rog's pants gave her an idea of why he groused, but she wondered why Hark did.

"You're right." Rog nodded. His face looked serious, but the expression didn't sit easy there. His face seemed made to laugh. Exuberance seemed to be the norm. On both of them. Smiles came easy from what she could see, and she wanted it to continue.

"Well, fine. But we do still have some time to explore. It's not like the dark would stop us. It's lit from within." Hark sounded a bit petulant.

Glancing at him, Grace laughed. Big puppy dog eyes, or should she say dragon eyes, fluttered, wide and begging.

Grace rubbed her nose against Rog's. "I guess we have time."

She really would like to explore more too. Lavinia and Paul's arrival detoured their afternoon plans. It didn't mean they couldn't still explore.

Rog slid her down his body grunting.

Grace gasped. Her sex quivered, the rest of her just wanted to feel him. Skin to skin. His hot hands caressing her body. Her mouth and tongue tracing his.

"Come on, you two." Hark griped.

Rog laughed. "Now I understand Ari and Crag."

"Who?" Grace breathed in his masculine scent.

"Our brothers. They have both found their mates. Now I understand." Rog rubbed his head on hers.

"Good, good. You understand. Now let's go." Hark headed toward the rear of the mine, turning into the room where the tunnel was hidden.

"We better catch up to him." Grace grabbed Rog's hand, pulling him after her.

He dragged his feet, tugging her closer to him. "Do we have to?" He chortled, mischief lighting his eyes. "Or we could just take advantage of him being gone."

Lord she needed a dip in the river. His smile, expression and touch blasted heat through her.

"Come on. Stop the kissy face." Hark's voice echoed.

Rog chuckled. His smile glowing from within. "Guess we better get going."

Grace giggled. Giggled. She'd never been so filled with delight. Her whole world suddenly seemed so much better. Brighter. Filled with a wonder she never expected. What she wouldn't give to spend a night in a bed with Rog.

She glanced at him from under her lashes. Her breath tangled in her throat. The lines of his body evident even with his clothing. Her heartbeat increased remembering the feel of his body pressed to hers. She wanted more.

His body, hers. Tangled together. Magnificent.

CHAPTER SEVEN

Room after room stored archaic machines. Some could be used, but most no longer filled a purpose. Unless human technology still functioned somewhere.

Rog was bored. Bored. Tired of finding nothing useful.

But, to his mate, to Grace, the rooms were a wonder. She exclaimed over each new thing she thought might be of use. Each expression of joy lightened his heart.

He was still bored though.

They didn't know if the whole world lost everything. They knew, from their dam and sire, the world suffered the same fate as this continent. Perhaps even here, some of the survivors were able to keep power on, run water plants, survive in some similar fashion to the past.

Looking up at the lighting, it dawned on him. Here the power was working. What kind, he didn't know. Flying over the mountains he'd not noticed anything resembling a power plant. But maybe, maybe, it was down here. Hidden under the mountain like this facility.

Perhaps this world could be made better. Not that he minded humans having lost the ability to fly. It made it safer for dragons. He knew the fire dragons survived. The ice dragons barely made it. They had a fighting chance now that the fire dragons had, for all intents and purposes, adopted them. Especially since most of them were children.

"You know, there is power down here." Rog spoke slowly. "Maybe some of this equipment can be used."

"Because the lights are working?" Grace stopped careening from item to item in yet another storeroom. She shrugged. "It's probably solar. We have them in my town. Doesn't mean anything that takes a lot of power can be used."

"Does each house provide its own power? Or are you on a grid?" Hark popped up, covered in dust, but wearing a big smile.

"Each house has a solar panel for power and heating water." Grace poked at a large piece of equipment. "There is a huge field of panels, but I just assumed they were surplus power for the town. I suppose they could be for here. No one ever said. We have no fossil fuels and even if we found them, no one knows how to refine them for use."

"True." Rog sighed. "But maybe we can find answers. Maybe the knowledge is down here to improve human lives."

"Why would we want to do that?" Hark gave him a disgusted look.

"Our mates are human." He raised his brow at his brother. "That's why."

"So, what. The world is once again clean and healthy. Think of how bad it was when we went to our last hibernation." He glanced around the room. "I'd destroy this all rather than let humans destroy the world again."

Rog stepped back, his jaw dropping. He struggled to find the right words.

Grace stepped quickly to Hark, placing a hand on his arm. "Then we won't let it out. At least nothing that would destroy the world again."

"Knowledge is power. The scars mankind left on the world are still here. I won't let it happen again if I can help it."

"Then we won't. We control this." Grace swirled in a circle, gesturing with an arm. "We do. Nothing has to make it back to my world."

Hark looked into her eyes, then grabbed her up in a hug.

Grace squealed.

With a grin, Hark set her down then patted her on the head. "You're a good egg."

"We're in this together. We all make decisions and have to agree before anything is moved from here." Rog glanced at each of them, waiting until they all nodded in agreement.

"To be honest," Grace sighed, "I don't want any of this brought to where my family lives. Somehow, some way, Lavinia's family would find a way to abuse it or hold it over the other families."

"That woman's family is in charge?" Hark sounded horrified.

Grace nodded.

Rog's lip curled. "How?"

Grace shrugged. "I don't know. They just always have been. It's why I don't live in town."

"Let's keep looking." Rog grabbed Grace's hands. Dusty but they fit perfectly in his.

"Actually, I'm hungry again." Hark's stomach took that moment to growl.

Grace giggled.

Rog shook his head, then his stomach followed suit. "Maybe we should go. We can block the door up top so no one finds it."

"I have a better idea." Hark strode passed them, heading to the door. "I'll stay here in the mine and you two can go back to Grace's soddy."

"It will take hours to get back there." Grace argued. "I don't want to walk through half the night."

"Not as the dragon flies." Rog thought Hark's idea was brilliant. "I can carry you. Just direct me. I bet it won't take more than a few minutes."

Her eyes lit up. "Really?" Grace nibbled on her lip. "Are you sure?"

"Positive." Rog couldn't wait to have her alone. His body hardened in anticipation. He sucked in a breath. He needed to calm down. He refused to change and fly with an erection.

"Let's eat first." Hark led the way rapidly from the facility. "I left a couple of buffalo in a nearby valley. I'll go get them."

Rog snorted. Of course, he had. His brother always thought of his stomach. He smirked. That led to his stomach being fed too. So it wasn't a bad thing.

Hark waited at the entrance. Rog and Hark placed the door back in place. Propped a couple of defunct pieces of equipment across it to hide it.

Grace looped her arm with his once it was completed.

Rog's heart swelled. He pulled her closer, enjoying the feel of her next to him. "Sounds good. I don't want to fly on an empty stomach."

"Will I be riding on your back?" Grace's eyes were wide. Excitement shown from them.

"No. In my talons. My spikes are too dangerous. They could cut you up."

Grace's face dropped. "Okay."

He wished he could give her a different answer. "When I change, check out my back. You'll understand then."

"Fine." Grace huffed.

Rog's heart lifted. Every emotion, every facet of her personality. Grace held back nothing. Her trust, and that is what it was, was gifted to him. He wasn't sure she even realized it. But he did. Rog leaned over and gave her a quick kiss.

She rolled her eyes but surrendered to it.

Rog couldn't suppress the smile in his kiss. Jumping from the quick bite of pain from Grace's pinch. Mercurial little thing. "Ow."

It got him the grin he expected. He always wanted to see her happy.

"I'm leaving. Don't mind me." Hark shifted into his dragon, leaping from the ledge, his clothes lying in a heap for his return.

Drama queen. Rog shook his head, Hark's laughter ringing in his head.

Hark's roar sent rocks skittering down the mountainside.

The fire lit the tunnel, illuminating the stark cavern. The contrast between the facility below and the reality of how far the humans had regressed was stark. Rog's throat thickened, thinking of how far they had fallen. All the lost possibilities his mate lost without even knowing.

"I want to put on a steak. Do you know where your brother put them?"

"I'll ask."

Where did you put Grace's steaks?

Further down the tunnel, the next opening past the room we found the locked door. It seemed colder there. I hid them from that woman.

Rog snickered. Lavinia definitely rubbed his brother the wrong way. *Thanks.*

"He left them in the next opening, past the locked door."

"Thank you." Grace scampered down the tunnel.

Rog admired the view. Her hips swayed calling his hands to hold them. He took a deep breath. Nothing would, could happen now. He thought of cold showers, his dam and sire and finally his erection subsided.

Plus, his brother would return shortly. And all their stomachs were demanding food. Even now, the biting ache in his belly called for food.

Grace returned. Arms full of silver bags. "I didn't think the food was too bad. What we found. I mean. It's hard to believe it's been down there well over a hundred years."

"We don't know their preservation methods."

"No. It just seems unlikely." Grace tossed a steak onto the fire, grabbing seasonings from her backpack and adding them. "I've been thinking. I don't want to leave here for the night. I don't want to waste any time exploring tomorrow. Surely there can't be that much more."

Rog kept his groan in. He'd hoped to persuade Grace into his arms for the night. "If you're sure." He didn't relish camping by the fire unable to touch her.

"I am. I'd like to stay in one of the rooms, if that's okay. I don't think there is any danger. It's deserted and has been for a long time." Her come hither look and shy smile froze him.

Did she mean what he thought she meant? "I could keep you company."

The blush inching up her face have him hope. "I'd like that."

That boner he'd suppressed popped back up. He stifled his moan. Just the thought of her, wrapped in his arms, testing one of the beds in the facility below sent his pulse racing. He thought of tasting the silk of her skin, sliding his hands over her curves.

"Here, I grabbed one for each of us." Hark dropped an animal at the entrance. "Please tell me we don't have to wait while Grace skins these."

Lost in his thoughts, he didn't realize Hark returned until the noise of his landing startled him from his imaginings.

"No, I'm hungry so you must be too. If I need to, I can always send you for more." She flashed a cheeky grin at Hark.

"Thank God. I'm going to eat at the ledge. Easier." He shifted again, flying out the mine. The terror filled lowing of the animal silenced.

"I'd better grab mine too. Before he eats them both." Rog ruffled Grace's hair, stripped, and shifted into his dragon following his brother.

***

Grace wandered around the living unit. After finishing supper, she and Rog headed back to the facility below. They left the fire burning, with Hark guarding the entrance. She didn't think it was necessary, but she didn't mind being alone with Rog.

She glanced at him from under her lashes. She pressed her hand against her belly, trying to settle the twisting and turning. Her neck and cheeks burned. She knew she was redder than anything. Rog turned her inside out. She fiddled with the hem of her shirt, smoothed it down. Did it again.

The silence ratcheted up her tension. She needed to break it before it broke her. "Do you think it's safe down here?"

"Yes."

"That's good." His one-word answer wasn't helping. Grace needed to occupy herself or she would just attack him.

She peeked at him again.

He tried to hide a grin beneath his palm.

She glared. "It's not funny." Darn it, he knew she was nervous.

Rog's teeth flashed. "It is, a little." He stood up from the couch he occupied. Coming closer until he loomed in her space. "Don't think about it."

She opened her mouth to give him a snarky response, but his mouth stopped her. Her brain circuits fried. The taste of him, the feel of his arms, drove her wild. Pressing closer, Grace slid her hands up his arms and around his neck. Stepping on tippy toes and drawing his head down.

Lips pressed and teeth clashed.

Rog's chuckle slid down her spine.

Her shiver woke up her nipples. They tingled and ached. Begging for Rog's touch, his mouth.

He seemed to know it. His mouth slid down her neck, tongue painting the way.

Her hands grasped his shoulders. She wanted to climb him, wrap herself around him.

His hands grabbed her, yanking her up, wrapping her legs around him. His hands slid into her waistband, sliding inside to cup her ass.

Grace trembled, gasping.

His rough hands kneaded her flesh, sending tingles over her body. One finger teased her opening.

She couldn't close against him. Didn't really want to. It felt too good.

His rough finger slid in and out, just a tip, teasing, tempting her.

She shuddered. Grace tugged at Rog's shirt, pulling it up and over his head, tossing it aside. She nuzzled his neck, slipping over to nibble on his ear.

His shudder sent satisfaction snaking through her.

Rog pulled one hand from her pants, moving it around to unbutton them. His hand slid inside, cupping her mound. His fingers sliding easily in her juices. Skimming her sensitive skin.

Her breath shuddered out of her. She quickly unbuttoned her shirt, shrugging it off. She dropped her legs.

His hands pushed her pants down. They whispered down her legs.

Her hands tugged at the waistband of Rog's pants, wrestling them from him.

She heard the plop of fabric hitting the ground. Then they stood, flesh to flesh. Her heart raced. Her breasts ached. Her nipples puckered against his hard chest. She rubbed her damp thighs together.

His hard length pressed insistently against her belly.

She peeked down. His darker flesh against hers. His hard to her soft. Her breath came in soft pants, almost a whine. She wanted, needed more. Butterflies swirled through her, accompanied by a rising tide of heat. Anticipation encompassed her from head to toe. Every press of her body against his burned even hotter.

Rog grabbed her, lips meshing against hers. Hard. Firm. Intoxicating.

Grace couldn't catch her breath. She didn't want to. She wrapped around him. Arms, legs, as close as she could. Drowning in his kiss.

Didn't matter he was a dragon. Grace knew he was her dragon.

Rog devoured her.

Her head spun. The room moved around her. Grace held on tight. Then she was falling, Rog on top, a soft surface beneath to stop her. The bedroom. Suddenly, Grace was conscious of the spread of her legs, the hard, insistent press of Rog's body poking hers.

He stilled. "Are you all right?"

Heat rose, from her toes to her cheeks. "Yes. Just…" Grace trailed off. She wanted him. Every part of him. But…

"I can just hold you." Rog sounded pained. His stiff cock at her entrance begged to be let in.

Grace giggled. She relaxed. The unknown fear leaving her body. Shifting her hips, she encouraged him. "No. I just, I don't know. I got scared for a moment." Wiggling, she tried to get Rog to move. "It's just new."

His body slid to her side. "New, new?"

Grace nodded. "Yup."

Rog's sly smile and the heat in his eyes told her he didn't mind at all. His hands roamed across her body, toying and tugging on her nipples.

Her breath sped up, lifting her chest into the air.

He leaned over, licking her nipples, his lips tugging at them.

An ache so good shot to her groin. She tried to close her legs, but his hands were there. Dancing around, teasing her. Dipping in and out, drawing out her wetness. One finger slid in, out, faster. Her hips rose.

Rog slid down, his face between her legs.

Goosebumps covered her.

His warm breath tightened her nerves. Then his tongue teased her.

Grace moaned, fingers grabbing at the mattress.

Rog nibbled. Added a finger. He twisted them, moved them faster, in and out.

Her breath stuttered.

He licked her. Tickled her. Suckled her clit.

Grace stiffened. Screamed when Rog sucked it harder. Warmth flooded from her. Her hips frantic on his fingers.

Rog pulled them out, sliding up her body. His cock slid into her. Stopped. Pushed forward. Seated himself fully in her.

The pinch of pain followed by his heat, burning her from the inside out. Filling her, stuffing her. Her body clenched his needing more.

Grace undulated, forcing movement. She groaned, it felt so good. She moved again, her movements limited, pressed down by the warm weight of Rog above her, in her.

"Fuck. I don't want to hurt you." His rough, hoarse voice did something to her.

She tightened on him, moaning at the sensation. "I need more. Move, please." Grace didn't care if sounded like she was begging. She needed this. More than food. More than air. "Please."

CHAPTER EIGHT

He couldn't deny her. Leaning down, devouring her mouth, Rog stole her breath. Pushing up, leaning on his arms, he looked down her body. Admiring the firm globes of her breasts. Her nipples dark pink from his playing. Her too slim belly, concaved inward. Dimpled by her sexy belly button.

Further down, the black curls guarding her treasure. The treasure he plundered.

His cock dove in, back out slowly. Covered in her juices and glistening in the light. Once more and Grace whined.

Her hands dug into his ass cheeks, trying to control him.

His dragon preened, his cock growing, stretching her.

Her pussy burned him, but in the best way. Warm, moist, clinging to him.

He never wanted to leave her. He thrust forward. Loving being engulfed in her body. He groaned. Hammered into her.

Grace wrapped her legs around him. Her hands feverishly roaming his chest and abs.

Fuck. He groaned.

Grace's lips suckled his nipple.

His breath hitched. A useless bit of flesh on a male, he'd thought.

The bite of her teeth forced a roar from his throat.

Burying his head in her neck, he bit down, holding her in place, more dragon than man.

His hips worked, slamming into her heat, her tight pussy calling to him.

Grace screamed, nails digging into his back, legs pulling him to her. Her passage strangling him, drowning him in the best way. Pulsing, tugging his own ejaculation from him.

Rog roared, jerking. His cum mingled with the Grace's. His cock emptying into her welcoming pussy.

He collapsed, deflating on top of Grace.

She groaned, hugging him to her.

Rog snuffled at her neck, kissing her. He knew he was heavy, but Grace's heavenly body against his was something he didn't want to give up.

Until she sighed, grunted, and tried to push him off.

Rog grunted. He rolled off her, and unfortunately slid out of her warm cocoon, groaning at the cool air on his penis. If he couldn't be on her, in her, he'd be as close as possible.

Grace snuggled back, her head on his arm, her arms around him.

Rog slid a leg over hers, pulling her even closer. He knew they couldn't cuddle forever. Grace's arm would lose circulation, but until then, it was nice. Better than. Her soft curves enticed him. Her body, his mate, was everything he could ever want. He couldn't keep his hands from roaming. He was spent but couldn't resist the silkiness of her skin.

Independent, spunky and intelligent, Rog thanked the powers that be for matching him with her.

Grace yawned, her jaw cracking. She pulled her arm out from under him, curling it between them. Wiggling until she found a comfortable position.

Rog encircled her. Arms, legs, all wrapped protectively around his mate.

Grace's breathing evened off. Little puffs of air against his shoulder slowed. Grace slept.

Content, Rog listened to her breathe.

The lights in the room began to dim. Rog watched as a feeble glow was left in the room.

His eyes adjusted to the darkness. Gazing around the spacious room, he could see himself living here. There was plenty of rooms. Room for Hark and his future mate. Room for any of Grace's family.

Not that nasty witch from earlier, though. Maybe even some of Hope's family. It would be good to bring some new blood into both of their lines. The segregation of both towns limited the bloodlines. One thing dragons knew were bloodlines.

Too much of the same blood lead to unhealthy people. Maybe one or two of his sisters might relocate here. Rog wondered if either of his sisters, Belissa and Juevatorj had found mates yet.

He gazed down at Grace. It only took a day to be completely besotted. If it hadn't happened to him, he wouldn't believe it.

He'd thought Ari crazy for hooking up with Hope so fast. Crag took more time, but only because he was afraid to tell Faith the truth.

Satisfaction slid through him. His mate, his Grace, knew the truth. He was a dragon. He would have to tell her about changing her into a dragon. He had time. He wanted to see if the facility they'd found was a good choice. The entrance to the mine to get here wasn't optimal.

Rog wondered where they could locate food. Dragon's needed more sustenance than the cattle they'd seen. Of course, there were the bigger ones. Buffalo. One made a good meal. But if humans became part of his entourage, they would need somewhere to grow food. Especially to survive in winter.

Seedlings could be started in the growing room they'd found. Rog didn't know if mature plants would survive there. Many of the items were no longer viable and would need to be scrapped.

They would have to finish exploring the facility. Hopefully tomorrow they would finish it all. Maybe even solve the mystery of why it remained empty of life.

Rog yawned. He should check in with Hark. *Everything okay up there?*

Fine. I'll get breakfast ready in the morning. Grab a couple of buffalo and something smaller for Grace. A couple of rabbits, maybe.

Do you think there is enough of the large animals to support a weyr here? Rog was curious what Hark's opinion was.

I think there is enough. If we were able to bring in more it would be better. Especially if we had to share the herd with humans. That is what you're asking, isn't it?

Yes. At least some humans.

Not that Lavinia woman. Hark spat her name.

No. Rog wondered what she'd done to have Hark bristle at her mention. *What did she do? To aggravate you so much?*

Complain and speak nastily about everyone she mentioned. Not just Grace and her brother, but everyone. Even her own brother wasn't spared. Her attitude could easily get her eaten. She wouldn't even sit by the fire. It was too dirty. She expected me to clean it. Hark snorted. *Not likely.*

What did you think of Grace's brother?

He seemed okay, but I would prefer to stay cautious. He is a human, after all.

I agree. Wake me if you need me. I'm going to get some sleep.

Rog yawned. His jaw cracked and his eyes watered. He snuggled close to Grace, breathing in her scent mixed with his. A smile tipped his lips and his breathing evened out. The only noise filling the room the sound of their breathing.

***

The tips of her ears warmed. Grace averted her gaze from Rog's body. One she'd explored in depth. Last night, and again this morning. Her eyes wandered back, checking out his rear end in his pants. She sighed. Her hands wanted to grab on and not let go.

Laughter tipped her head up.

"I'd hoped not to see any of that." Hark's snicker ushered heat into her cheeks.

"Shut up." Obviously, he knew Rog and she became intimately acquainted last night.

Rog grinned. Sauntering over to Grace, Rog slid an arm around her waist, squeezing her tight. "Disregard him. He's just jealous."

Hark rolled his eyes. "I'd just like to finish exploring."

Face red, Grace wanted to sink into the floor. But the warmth of Rog against her side anchored her. Hark was correct, though. They needed to finish exploring.

"He's right. Let's finish exploring. I'd like to see what is down here before anyone else comes nosing around, wondering what I'm doing." Grace wiggled out from under Rog's shoulder.

She made it as far as her hand.

Rog refused to let go. Pulling her back in for a kiss.

Grace melted against him. Ignoring the grumbles from Hark. Heat seared her from head to toe. She was ready to toss exploring away when Rog eased back. Breathless, Grace inhaled a shuddering breath.

Rog's mouth quirked.

Grace shook her head, a smile teasing her lips. "You make me lose my mind."

"Me too. Come on, you two." Hark's exaggerated gag pulled a giggle from Grace.

Rog just grinned. "Fine, let's continue."

They passed the rooms from yesterday, Grace behaving and only giving a yearning glance at the rooms she'd like to delve into further, like the growing room, and the room filled with seeds. Her curiosity demanded a thorough examination of everything.

A few of the rooms were filled with laboratories and computers. The equipment whose knowledge to use no longer existed in her world. At least, not in the town she grew up in.

Room after room filled with items she had no knowledge of. Her chest tightened. Seeing what the world once held, her eyes ached and her sinuses stung. Her world could have been so much bigger. Not so hard to survive.

The signs on the doors gave some idea of what to expect inside. Medical supplies that still could be used. A library filled with more books than she'd ever seen. Science laboratory, and inside still more doors. Doors that they left closed. Virus development, cloning development, weapons development. Doors that needed to be locked if not destroyed.

They all looked at virus development and backed away. They recognized whatever existed behind that door could once again destroy the world.

Grace's stomach dropped. "That can never happen again. No one needs to go in there. Not ever."

Rog and Hark, more solemn then she'd ever seen them nodded in agreement.

"We will make sure." Rog slipped his hand into hers. "We can seal the doors."

"Take the name off of it." Hark looked at it. "Or cover it up."

"Put a hazard marking on it. Then no one would go in." Grace added.

"No. That would only draw attention to it." Rog sighed. "Someone would be curious."

"Can we seal it now?" Grace tightened her fingers, weaved together with Rog's.

"Sure." Hark strode over to the door, examining it. "Rog what do you think?"

Rog released Grace's hand, joined his brother. "I don't even want to open it." He pointed at the door and the frame. "This should be easy enough."

Hark looked around the room, grabbed a stool and brought it back. "This would make it easier."

Rog nodded. He and Hark tore it apart.

Hark held the tube of the leg against the crack of the door and frame. His hands covered in dragon scales.

Grace stared in fascination.

Rog's face morphed, changing to look more dragon than man. Then he opened his mouth. Fire, blue and obviously hot, shot out. Melting the leg, filling in the cracks around the door. He continued, taking a breath when a new piece needed to be put in place.

Grace focused, mesmerized. The whole scene in front of her was compelling. The abilities held by the dragons more than she'd ever imagined.

The frame and door plus the seal the men, dragons, dragon men, forged glowed red. The heat obvious.

Hark flicked his finger against it, nodding in satisfaction. He blew against the door, the paint of the letters melting off.

Hark and Rog stepped back. Looked at the door.

Rog grasped the handle, broke it off. Taking another piece of the chair, he held it in place, blew more flame, sealing the surface, leaving no handle to even open it.

"There." He stepped back, ran his claw over the seal, the handle area. Even the door hinges were melted, no differentiation between them and the rest of the frame. "No one should ever be able to get inside now. At least not without a lot of effort."

Grace nodded. "What about the other doors?"

Hark frowned. "Weapons development should be sealed too. Rog?"

"I agree." He grabbed another stool, tore it apart. Held the leg against the door.

Hark morphed, and repeated Rog's actions, sealing the door against any intrusion.

"What about the clone development?" Grace frowned.

"Do you know what that is?" Rog walked over to it.

"No." Grace walked over to the door. "Should we open it?"

"No. Let's keep going. We can explore in depth later." Rog quirked a brow at Hark.

"You're right. We only had a couple more doors to explore." Hark headed out. "Let's go."

Rog grabbed Grace, hauled her against him. He'd shifted back to looking like a human.

Grace was now aware to her bones that he wasn't human. She wrapped her arms around him, tilting her head up for his kiss. But whatever, he was hers. Happiness fluttered in her chest. Hers.

"Enough." Hark's hand tugged Rog from her embrace. "Let's finish."

Rog kept his arms around her, dragging her with.

Grace giggled. She never giggled, but these brothers brought a joy to her life she'd never had. She couldn't stop smiling. Grace tumbled after them, kept on her feet by Rog's hold.

"Just a few doors left." Rog stared at the end of the corridor in front of them.

Grace looked. "One says cryonics. One says stairs."

The third and final door loomed over them. Huge, it had a window that was darkened. No light shown through it.

Rog and Hark headed straight to it. Poked around, grunted trying to lift the bottom, and suddenly the door rumbled and rose in the air. They stepped quickly back.

Grace hurried to join them. Her jaw dropped, the vista from the door unexpected. Excitement swirled in her belly. "Look."

Hark and Rog sported grins across their faces. All three of them walked forward. Stopped at the entrance. Boulders filled most of the tunnel, but not all. Not the view meeting their eyes.

Grace gazed, taking everything in. Mountains surrounded a beautiful valley. Green and lush. It looked like it went on forever. Animals grazed in the distance. Horses, cattle, even buffalo. The mountains had goats, sheep and, she thought, donkeys. Most of the animals ignored the noise of the door opening. Perhaps they were too far away to notice.

"Let's explore." Hark stripped, dropping his clothes. He ran forward, around any boulders in his way. Once clear he shifted, his wings driving him into the air.

"Shall we?" Rog held out a hand, ushering her before him. A charming grin and the excitement sparkling in his eyes convincing her.

"Yes."

They walked hand in hand around the debris. Once Grace pulled her hand away and passed Rog, she turned and watched his transformation. His dragon as handsome as the man. She pressed a hand to her chest. Her eyes ate up every detail.

The dragon preened, expanding his chest, stretching out his neck.

He was beautiful. Coal dark, golden eyes. In the sunlight, his scales shimmered. A touch of red flickered under the black with each movement.

Grace approached slowly. His eyes, Rog's eyes, never left her. Holding out her hand, he nuzzled her. Joy burst over her. She hugged his neck, ran a hand over his legs, examined his back. She remembered what he said. She checked his spines. Unless she wanted to be speared to death, there would be no riding on his back.

His talons it was.

"Okay, how does this work?" Grace stood back, looking at him.

Rog ran forward, his wings propelling him up. He banked, hovered over her, offering his hand, claw, or talon, she wasn't sure what to call it, to her.

Grace climbed in. She had plenty of room. How a large man transformed into such a huge creature she didn't know. Magic. It was the only thing that made sense.

Rog closed his talon around her, leaving room for her to look out.

Grace couldn't stop the thrill from running through her. They rose higher, flew forward. Flew. She was flying. Looking out, seeing the land unfold before her, awe filled her. A grin spread across her face. Her hands grasped Rog's talons, holding on to see everything. She was flying!

CHAPTER NINE

Rog could feel Grace's hands holding on to him. Pride filled him at her courage.

She whooped. Her excitement palpable.

Rog's heart glowed. His mate, everything he could ever want. He looked over the valley. Larger than expected, it teamed with life. Animal. No touch of humans remained. A couple of spots that once upon a time could have been some type of human habitat. Covered over now by nature. They flew past a lake. A river led to it, and from it.

From the telltale jumping, and circles left behind, it was filled with fish. It was a perfect habitat. Too perfect. Obviously, manmade. It was large enough the animals grazing didn't compete for food. The rivers strategically placed to separate the divergent species. There was room for crops. Animals lived in abundance. With a careful husbandry schedule, even dragons could live here happily.

It's perfect. Rog gazed over it all. Thinking of a life here with his mate. His brother.

We could live here. Hark sighed happily. *It has everything we could ever need.*

It's far enough away from the main weyr. We wouldn't be stretching resources. Rog knew that was important. Spreading out a bit would ensure they wouldn't die out or die from an unexpected attack.

Not too far for visits either. Hark's excitement was catching.

Close enough for Grace to have her family near. If she wants.

Safe to fly. There is no one here to even see us.

Except those we choose to live here with us. Satisfaction oozed from Rog's words. He could envision living here with his mate, his hatchlings spreading their wings in a safe environment. *Let's do it.*

Agreed. Now let's see everything that now belongs to us.

Rog roared his agreement.

The sound of their dragons echoed back from the mountains. The animals below froze recognizing their supremacy. All in all, it was the best of days.

Let's head back. Check out the last two doors. Rog arced, turning back toward the facility.

Hark roared in agreement, banking near the base of the mountain, skimming over the trees to return.

They flew, side by side. Gliding on thermals in the air, checking out the fertile land below.

Rog hovered near the door, releasing Grace slowly.

She tumbled out, a grin gracing her face. Joy emanated from her. "That was fantastic."

Rog settled down, shifting. He grabbed his clothes, dressing quickly. Hauled her into his arms. Enjoying the warmth of her, the softness of her curves against him.

Hark landed behind Grace, shifted and dressed. Rolled his eyes, but the smile across his face leaving Rog in no doubt he shared their happiness. "Let's finish checking this place out. Plus clear a better path to go in and out."

Rog breathed in the scent of Grace's hair. He could hold her forever. But she was pulling back, eager to finish the last of their cursory investigation.

Grabbing her hand, weaving their fingers together, Rog bussed Grace on her forehead. "Almost done."

They headed in. "Stairs or cryonics?" Hark waved at the doors, offering a choice.

"Stairs seem self-explanatory. Let's see what cryonics are." Grace tugged her hand free, heading toward the door. She opened it, quickly entering. Her gasp had Rog racing to her.

"Oh." Rog stopped behind her, pulling her against him.

Hark slid next to him. "What the hell?"

Rog's stomach turned at the sight of rows of people in what looked like coffins. Lights blinked around them. Squares with numbers and letters scrolled across a screen at each… unit.

"Do," Grace cleared her throat. "Do, you think they are alive?" She walked forward, touching the glass surrounding one of the bodies.

Rog and Hark looked at each other and shrugged.

"Maybe?" Rog joined her, pressing his hand against the glass.

"Now we know what happened to all the people that lived here." Hark shook his head. "What a shame."

Grace traced letters on one case. It had a sign on it.

Rog wandered over. "What did you find?"

"Look." Grace shook her head. "Wake up procedure. Start here. Follow the directions exactly." Her frown grew. "It seems to be steps. Directions."

"Shall we?" Rog read the directions. "Seems to be easy enough."

"What are you talking about?" Hark was staring into one of the coffins. "What did you find?"

"I think it is directions to wake up the people here." Grace's voice trembled. "Do you think we should?"

Rog looked around. If they woke up all the people successfully, they would fill the facility they found. But they obviously had planned on living here. Probably had built it. He bit his lip, debating.

Do you think we should try? If we succeed, we probably won't be able to live here. Rog liked what they had found, but he didn't build it. It belonged to these people. He gazed around at the all the coffins. Maybe they weren't coffins. Maybe they really could bring them back to life.

I'd be okay with that. Who knows if it will work? If they were preserved around the time of the apocalypse, they may not have had the technology to know if it would work. It could have just been a last-ditch effort. Hark ambled closer, looking over Grace's shoulder.

"Can you imagine if they wake up? What knowledge they will have?" Grace's eyes were huge. "I wonder what they will think of the world now. Can you imagine how different it will seem to them?"

"I take it you think we should try." Rog tugged her into his arms. He would do as she preferred. She, after all, was still human. For the moment. "But I have a question for you first. Would you like to become a dragon?"

"What?" Grace's head snapped up, staring into his eyes. The sparkle in her eyes, the smile growing on her lips gave her answer. But he needed to hear it.

"Will you become a dragon, like me? Stay with me. For all of our long lives." Rog tensed. Maybe he wouldn't tell her exactly how she would be changed. He could see his brothers reasoning for not telling their mates exactly how it would happen.

"Is it painful?" Grace's question startled a laugh from him.

"No. Not at all." Rog nuzzled her neck, whispering in her ear. "It's extremely pleasurable."

Grace sighed, tilting her head back. "If it doesn't hurt." She wound her arms around his neck. "I would like nothing more. Love nothing more. But why the rush?"

"Because if for some reason these people attack, you'd survive. If you change, then I'll never lose you. You would learn to fly. To soar. You'd have none of the weakness of a human." Rog's pulse sped. Thinking of Grace, her scales gleaming in the sun, the wicked twinkle in her eyes while he chased her. He breathed deep, trying to settle down. They needed to be outside. He whispered. "You'll be even sexier than you are now." He would need more dragons to change her. Just himself and Hark wouldn't be enough.

Even though the thought brought his dragon wanting to wrap protectively around her. He'd never been good at sharing. But he knew that once his pheromones called to her, signaled the other dragons nearby, nothing but changing and claiming her would matter.

"Now?" Her body plastered to his.

His body stirred, dragon rising.

"No. We should try to wake these people. Unless you two intend on getting busy surrounded by all these people. Even if they are asleep." Hark touched a tank. "Or dead. That would be worse, I'd think."

Hark's words cooled his ardor. The idea of changing Grace in such an atmosphere left him cold.

"Let's see if we can wake them." Rog released Grace from his arms. Running a finger down her silk soft cheek. "Then we'll make you mine."

Her pout tempted him to change his mind. "Fine."

"Let's do this. Start here. I'm assuming this means with him." Hark read out the directions.

Grace and Rog crowded around the container. She stood to the left and Rog took the right. They followed the directions, carefully following each move read out.

Lights blinked, the liquid holding the body changing color. Gasses leaked out.

Rog could tell they weren't harmful, but he wrinkled his nose at the stink.

The readout at the base of the container continued to scroll information, changing faster than he could keep up with.

Some of the steps requiring a certain amount of time to pass. With no way to tell, they took turns counting out loud. Hopefully it was enough. They tried.

"That's it." Hark stepped back.

"Now what?" Grace frowned, moving next to Hark to stare at the body.

"No clue." He tapped the glass. Nothing happened.

Rog stared at the body. "Maybe it takes time." His stomach growled. "How about we grab some lunch?" He glanced at Grace winking at her. "And maybe while we wait, we can see about that dragon thing?"

A smile lit her face. "Now that sounds like a great idea."

You know that might not be the best idea right now. Hark rolled his eyes.

Why? Rog growled. His mind wholly engrossed with stripping Grace. Making her his.

If they wake up while we are otherwise occupied, they could kill us. We have no idea of what they are capable of.

Damnit. He hated when his brother was logical.

Hark chuckled.

"What?" Grace looked between them.

"My brother just reminded me that wasn't the best idea. If we were changing you, and these people woke up, we wouldn't want to be surprised by them." Rog snarled. Just the thought brought out his dragon.

"Well, then let's get something to eat." Grace slipped her hand into his.

Her warm hand, fingers entwined with his, settled him.

***

"Fine." Rog's fingers tightened around hers. His stomach growled, bringing a smile to her face.

Her belly fluttered, thinking of how Rog would change her. He hadn't said anything to make her think it, but if just sex changed her, it would have happened last night. She hadn't missed his references to we. She looked at Hark under her lashes.

His features were just as handsome as Rog's, but he didn't send butterflies winging in her belly. Maybe she was wrong, but becoming a dragon seemed awesome and she'd do whatever Rog needed to be like him. Even if it meant *that.* But feeling the twinge between her legs, maybe waiting a bit would be a good thing.

"Food sounds good." She snuggled into him. "Give the man a chance to wake up. If he's going to."

"You don't think all of them will wake up?" Rog glanced down at her.

"No. Only the container we worked on did anything. If he wakes, maybe he will wake the rest." She took a deep breath, slipping by Rog to go outside. She dragged him behind her, not releasing his hand.

"If he wakes. What if they don't?" Hark turned, walking backward.

The wind ruffled his dark hair, cut shorter than Rog's, but didn't flow around him. The green of the grass behind him outlined the hardness and largeness of his body. His eyes shown gold, glee gleaming from them. His features, similar to Rog's, even in repose showed laugh lines.

Grace couldn't help but like him. She didn't want more though.

Glancing at Rog, remembering the feel of his muscles pressed against her, heated her blood. His hair, shoulder length, stirred around his head. Her fingers longed to tangle amongst his strands again.

"Then we either seal that room or burn them." Rog looked down at her. His eyes burned, looking straight into her soul. The desire in his eyes heating her blood, sending tingles through her body.

She could lose herself in his eyes, his soul. "Wait. What? Burn them?"

"If they don't wake up. Whatever we did will change the chemicals, I'd bet. Eventually the bodies will decompose. And what if they were infected by whatever diseases were caused by the apocalypse? Maybe they were put there for some future cure."

"Why didn't you mention that before? We could just have destroyed humans again without knowing." Hark yelled, his voice changing into a deep growl. He shifted without notice, crowding Rog and her against the door they'd just come out of. "Fuck."

Her heart sank hearing Rog's words. It never crossed her mind. That the humans from the past could be carrying diseases. Potentially killing the rest of her race off. Grace watched Hark turn and fly off. She could hear the frustration in his roars. "God, I hope not." She grasped Rog's arm squeezing it. "Do you really think that?"

Rog shrugged. "I don't know, but it is a possibility. What if this place was hidden because of just that reason?"

Grace pressed a hand against her heart. Her nose stung, thinking of the devastation they might have unknowingly released. She whispered. "I pray you're wrong."

"So do I." Rog bowed his head. "So do I."

Grace's stomach growled. She didn't have much of an appetite though. Thinking of eating made her a bit queasy.

"We still need to eat. I'll grab a bite and see if I can grab you something small." Rog stripped of his clothes, shifting. His dragon nuzzled her, blowing her hair around her head.

Grace laughed. Raised her hands, smoothing them along his face. "Go eat. I'll see if I can find some eggs. Or I can grab a chicken. It'll be enough for lunch and dinner."

Rog nodded, turned and flew off.

Grace could still hear Hark.

His fierce roars seemed almost mournful. He flew beyond her sight, deep in the valley spread around her.

Sending up a prayer to a God she'd never believed in, Grace could only hope her discovery didn't mean the end of her world.

There was nothing she could do — her stomach protested — except eat and hope. Grace saw a structure where the chickens congregated. Block walls crumbled together, but a small opening showed the birds going in and out. She ducked inside. Blinking, she looked around. Once upon a time it must have been something to see. Three rows of metal shelves lined the walls. Most were dark and empty crumpled together under the weight of block. Broken bits of the walls littered the ground. Only a few shelves held nesting materials. A few bins held eggs. She wouldn't dare eat them. Grace blew air from her nostrils, trying to clear the smell. She backed out of the coop. The animals lived in the wild. The coop stank of feces and decomposition.

Turning to the yard, she spotted a group pecking at the ground. Walking slowly to them, Grace leaned over.

The birds squawked, feathers ruffling a bit. Grace grinned. They weren't afraid of her. They didn't even bother to run. Looking around, seeing the animals within sight Grace figured someone was looking out after the livestock. They wouldn't have stayed here without food. They would have wandered away or become food to predators.

Slowly, to keep them from flying off, she lowered her hands on either side of one of the big rust and white colored hens. She quickly grabbed it and straightened up. She easily dispatched the chicken.

Sitting on a rock near the stream Grace dunked the chicken and skinned it. Not wanting to deal with a big mess, she cut off the breasts, wings and legs. She set the rest aside to bury later.

Grace sat, checking the sky. No dragons were in view yet. Their coal black forms were obvious in the sky. But from a distance they looked like crows. Excitement swirled inside. She could hardly wait to fly the skies next to Rog.

Holding onto his leg and looking down at the green land beneath them had been wonderful. Soon enough she'd be able to fly. A thrill ran through her. Her, flying. Grace had seen pictures of airplanes in books. Nothing like that existed anymore. Nothing that took drilling for fossil fuel.

Their school in town covered the history of before and after the apocalypse. Grace thought a lot of it was exaggerated until she'd toured the facility she'd found. She hoped the people they found in the cryonics container weren't disease carriers.

If they woke up, she wondered what they would think of the world now. Would they be shocked? Would they bring knowledge lost to the past back? Would they be peaceful, or would they become a drain on her world?

She had so many unanswered questions.

"You're deep in thought." Rog's words behind her sent her jumping.

Grace pressed a hand to her beating heart. "You surprised me. I didn't hear you come back." She glanced around. "Did your brother come back?"

"Yes. He went to grab some pants."

Grace bit her lip, heat sliding up her cheeks. "That's good." She'd prefer if he came back dressed. They didn't seem to mind walking around without clothes, but it wasn't something she was used to. She pressed her hands against her hot cheeks. Thinking about Rog naked raised her temperature again.

Rog laughed and kissed her on her nose.

She giggled and wrinkled it at him. "What's that for?"

"You're cute when you're red." He moved to the fire pit. "Let me get the fire going so you can cook your chicken. That is chicken, isn't it?"

"Yes." She nodded. "Did you eat already?"

"Uh huh. Easier as a dragon." He got the fire going, a smolder, then flames shooting up. He sat down on the ground, lounging next to the fire. His muscular body stretched out, relaxed across the grass.

Once the flames settled down a bit, Grace found a rock she could use to cook on. Poking a bit of the fire away, she cleared a spot in the embers, then tossed one of the breasts and a leg onto it. The sizzle and pop of the meat cooking wafted under her nose. Glancing around, she spied some wild herbs.

Grace gathered a sprig of rosemary. Squishing it a bit to send a bit of aroma out, she tore it into two pieces. Grace placed the sprigs over each piece. She sat next to Rog. Scooching over to sit side by side with him.

Hands tugged her down, pulling her backwards.

With a squeal, she landed on her back, Rog leaning over her with a grin. "I missed you."

Grace smiled, wrapping her arms around his neck. "I missed you too."

"How about me? Did you miss me?" Hark flopped down on his back next to her.

Making Grace a sandwich between the two muscular men. Heat streaked from her head to toe. Both of their bodies radiated heat, making her blood boil and tightening her nipples. Maybe she wasn't too sore.

CHAPTER TEN

Rog could smell the pheromones emanating from Grace. He'd worried about making her sore. From her slightly different gait this morning he knew she had to be. Her smile told a different story.

Now, she called to the dragon in him.

She didn't seem bothered about Hark being right beside her.

Rog admitted to a sneaking suspicion she guessed what he failed to tell her.

Grace nibbled on his ear. "If the people inside wake up and I'm still human and they carry diseases, won't I die?"

Rog stilled.

His brother gaped at Grace.

"Well?" Her breath blew across his ear.

He shuddered. His dick lengthened. His pheromones spread, reacting to the scent her body exuded. Changing on the wind. Calling for assistance to change his mate.

Her wiggle, fitting him in her cleft just made him hungrier.

"Maybe." He couldn't bear the thought. After just finding Grace, Rog refused to lose her.

"Probably." Hark added. He rolled to his side, watching Grace intently and traced the edge of her ear with a fingertip.

"Then maybe the two of you should do what you need to make me a dragon." Grace purred.

Rog grinned. Yes, his mate was a smart one. "Well, it might take more." He licked down her neck, teasing her.

"More what?" She groaned, arching into his touch.

"More than two dragons to change you." Hark growled.

Glancing at his brother Rog realized Hark was responding to their combined pheromones. Hark slipped off his clothes, stretching out next to them. He didn't touch Grace except with a fingertip. Hark ran it down her neck, across her top, tracing the nipples that shown through her top and down.

Rog groaned. He gripped Grace's shirt, pulling it over her head, tossing it away. Rog slid down, tongue driving a path to a nipple. Suckling, he worked it. Rolling and nipping it until it blossomed into a hard nub.

He shoved her pants down, tearing them off along with his. He kissed down her stomach, circling her belly button, his tongue dipping inside. Kissing the curve below it. Breathing deep, he licked the crease of her thighs.

Grace opened, spreading her legs farther apart. Arching to capture his mouth. He stroked lightly over the petals of her sex, spreading her. Tickling her bundle of nerves.

Her whine inflamed his senses.

Glancing up, Rog admired the flush of her rosy skin, the jiggle of her breasts. Her raspberry colored nipples begged to be tasted. Instead, he buried his head in her sex. Teasing and nipping, licking the honey pouring from her.

Rog sank his tongue inside, nose nuzzling her clit.

A squeal broke from her.

A glance showed Hark greedily suckling at her teat. His other hand tugging her other nipple.

Rog slid his hands beneath her buttocks, angling her toward his mouth. He feasted.

A stirring of wind behind him told him another dragon was close enough to answer the mating call. A bugle in the air, heralded a fourth dragon before the air near them stirred again.

Rog glanced up. Not an ice dragon, thank goodness. Looked like the blond, blue eyed man was an air dragon. The other, brown hair and green eyes could be either a water dragon or an earth dragon. What mattered is their answer to the call.

"Zeru." The blond nodded at Rog, sliding down to take possession of one of Grace's breasts from Hark.

"Indra." The rough voice belonged to the darker man. He sat on his knees, his hands delving in Grace's hair, tracing her eyes. "Haven't heard of a mating in years."

Rog grunted, busy savoring Grace and listening to her squeals.

Grace thrashed between them, sucking in air and whining, pleading for more. Her head whipped to the side, Indra's cock slapping against her cheek. Grace arched her neck, mouth open, seeking. She latched on his cock, sucking.

His groan goaded the rest of them.

Feverishly, they caressed, nibbled and sucked on Grace. Her nipples stood twisted and hard in the air. Hands slid around her, plumping her breasts. Tweaking her nipples. Spots of red covered her skin, blood rising to the surface from the mouths cascading over her.

Rog pulled back, admiring her swollen pussy. Red and glistening, begging to be filled. Rog slid a finger, then two into her. She raised her hips begging for more.

A hand slid down, spreading her juices, swirling further down. Circled her anus, slid inside and back out, going deeper each time.

Another slid to caress her clit, teasing it, flicking it.

Grace moaned, spreading her legs further.

Rog's fingers were covered in her dew. He added another finger, stretching her tight passage.

Fingers pushed back the hood covering her clit. Hark slid in, blocking Rog's view. Sucked her clit.

Grace arched. Her pussy squeezed his finger, drawing them deeper. Her scream echoed across the valley. Wetness gushed from her, covering his fingers.

Cock aching, Rog pushed away the others. Drilling his cock into her tight passage he pounded. He swelled larger than ever, throbbing, ready to release.

Hands pulled him back. Pushed him over.

Eyes flashing, Rog growled.

"Not yet." Hark's hoarse voice penetrated his brain.

Rog turned, diving to sip at her nipples, eyes trained on her pussy. His pussy.

A cock sunk inside her, banging her. Rog slid his hand down, playing with his pussy. His. Circling again and again on her clit until she broke.

Convulsing on the cock in her.

Another grunt, another hand yanking away a body and another cock pushed into Grace. Cum spurted over her belly, coating her stomach and over her exposed nipple.

Rog's mouth worked, sucking her tit. Closing his eyes to keep from getting any cum in them. His hand roamed her pussy, teasing, touching, claiming.

Grace squirmed frantically. Her juices spread down her thighs, lubricating the rotating cocks pumping into her.

Rog flipped her over onto her belly. Slid underneath her. Speared her with his throbbing cock. Pulled her forward, exposing her ass to the air.

Someone took the challenge. Slowly filled her ass.

Grace hissed, whined.

Rog rubbed her back. Hands joined his, caressing her.

Grace wiggled, seating firmly on Rog. Pushing the cock in her ass to the hilt.

Rog groaned. He never thought Grace could get any tighter. He looked up.

Blue eyes looked down; mouth drawn in a hiss. Scales rippled across his features. He drove into Grace. Gritted his teeth and withdrew. Repeated it, moving easier with each thrust.

Hands roamed Grace's skin, soothing her, tracing her body.

Rog waited, pumped. Grabbed Grace's hips. Lifted and dropped her. Counter point to Zeru. Soon enough, the fire rose in Rog. The burning need to envelope Grace in his fire. Engulf her in his flames, spread it until her dragon emerged.

Zeru groaned, gritted his teeth and pulled out. His cock pulsed, cum spraying across Grace. Hands rubbed it in, making her skin glow.

Grace howled, convulsed on his cock.

He swelled, her passage constricting him, pulling him deeper.

Rog roared, his seed pulsing from him, filling Grace.

Food, we'll need lots of food! He should have prepared.

***

Fire filled her, engulfing her body.

Rog thrummed inside her. Stream after stream filling her body.

Their groins sliding and slipping in the sticky mess.

Her body throbbed. Satiation filled her senses. Grace relaxed, sprawled across Rog's musclebound form. Her nipples ached. Her sex pulsed. She wiggled, enjoying Rog's cock still filling her pussy.

A slight breeze flowed over her. Cooling her senses. A twinge brought a frown. Fire raced in her blood. Grace shivered, not from cold but from heat.

Hands soothed her, murmuring in her ear.

"She'll need food." Rog's sexy voice was hoarse.

"We'll hunt, bring enough for all of us."

Grace didn't recognize the voice that spoke. She cracked an eye. All she saw was muscular buttocks striding away, then a blue dragon that disappeared before her eyes. She blinked. Then snuggled back into Rog's chest. She decided she must be hallucinating, and ignored it.

"I restart the fire, then hunt." Another voice she didn't recognize. This time she didn't even bother to look.

She counted. Four men, four dragons to turn her. If it worked. "Did it work?" God, she hoped it worked. She barely got the words out. Her throat dry, hoarse from screaming and pleading. She winced. Her body ached. It was such a good ache, though. Heat spread under her skin, probably accompanied by her skin turning pink as usual. She wasn't sure she'd be able to look the others in the eye.

Rog slid from her.

Fluids gushed from her body. Grace rolled onto her back, the cool of the ground a relief. Wonderful as Rog was, he was hot. His body temperature akin to a roaring furnace. She whimpered. The ache was intensifying, running through her, from her womb out. From her skin in.

Rog picked her up. "It's okay. You're just changing."

Changing, hell. Fire tore through her body. Pulled a gasp from her. She was burning up. "Hot."

Water splashed. Rog eased them both into the river. Cradled her in his arms.

The cool water eased the pain in her groin. Delicious pain, but pain none the less. Grace sighed, relaxing in Rog's loose embrace. Another wave of heat took over her body. Her hands convulsed on his arms.

"It's okay. Shouldn't be long before it's done." Rog kissed the top of her head. His arms moved, letting her legs fall across his lap. His hands ran across her body, soothing the fire filling her.

"Are you sure?" Grace sure hoped so. Her belly churned. Whether it was from her body changing or excitement, it was hard to say. The idea of being able to fly, soaring across the world. Grace shivered, anticipation filling her. If this was as bad as it got, she had this.

"Yes. My brother's mates didn't seem like it was too long before they shifted." Rog kissed the top of her head.

His sweet gesture melted her.

Grace molded herself to his side. The smell of roasted meat drifted to her. She lifted up her head, taking a deep breath. Underneath that, the smell of burnt meat assaulted her nose. "Oh no. I forgot about the chicken in the fire."

Rog laughed. "Don't worry. Indra put a meat on the fire, then went for more. Hark and Zeru are also hunting."

"Who are... never mind." How many times could her cheeks burn? Shouldn't there be a limit? Zeru and Indra must be the other dragons that answered the call. Speaking of which, she never heard Rog call out. "I never heard you call asking for help. Did you get on a dragon hot line or something?"

"No." He grinned at her. "When it is time to mate, I send out pheromones from my body. They interact with yours. When they combine, the scent travels on the wind. The nearest unmated dragons answer the call."

"Oh." That was more than she wanted to know. Her body odor called them. Ugh. "Wait. Does that mean whenever we have sex, others will be called?" She couldn't help the dismay from coloring her tone. Even though the sex was intense, she didn't want to have to watch where they had it if it called others to join in.

"No." The amusement in his tone barely deserved a glare. "It only happens the once, when our mates need to be changed into a dragon."

"Thank god. I think it would kill me if it happened more than once."

Rog's chuckle made her brain want to slap him, but her body's contentment decided it wasn't worth the effort. She settled for a snort.

Her eyes widened. Smoke lingered in the air. "Did I just do that?" Smoke, from her nose. Awesome. She did it again, tickled pink at the same result.

Rog's belly laugh brought a giggle from her.

"I did, didn't I? I guess it worked." A wave of heat flowed through her. Intensified, then eased. "Maybe it's not quite done yet."

"Soon. I don't think it gets any worse. Hope and Faith seemed to weather it okay."

"Who are they?" Her voice sharpened. He better not have anyone else he'd made a mate. "You don't have a harem, do you?" She wouldn't stand for that. Maybe she should have made sure before she allowed him to touch her.

"My brother's mates. Ari is mated to Hope and Crag is mated to Faith. The two women are sisters." Rog nuzzled her temple. "Dragons don't have harems. One is enough for us."

"Good." Grace relaxed. The smell of meat drifted to her again. A voracious greed lit her belly. She blinked. Her view changed, becoming sharper. A roar filled her head. She needed to feed. She rolled over, intent on sating her hunger.

She growled at the male standing over the meat.

He looked up and backed away. Smart man.

Grace grabbed the meat, pulling it from the fire and devoured it. It wasn't enough. Swinging her head, nose lifted to scent, she arrowed in on a pile. The iron filled richness of blood called to her. Engrossed in the craving, the need filling her, Grace headed straight toward it. Two males stood too close.

Roaring, she charged, chasing them away. Circling her bounty, Grace dug in.

She ignored the males nearby. They were in no danger unless they dared try to take her meal away.

CHAPTER ELEVEN

Rog watched his mate shift. He didn't think she even realized it. He heard her stomach growl and then a dragon appeared in her place.

I hope you have more coming. Rog knew Hark had witnessed a change before. Knew how hungry a new dragon was.

Of course, I do. Indra and Zeru are getting more also.

Remember, don't hold anything back for yourselves.

Harks chuckle had him grinning. *Oh, I remember.*

Rog grinned. He was the fool the first time. Figuring Hope was full, he'd decided to grab a bite for himself. He was lucky he was still alive.

A dragoness's bite was venomous. Admittedly he had an advantage. He'd grown some immunity from bites since his sisters tended to bite first to win in any type of altercation. But he'd still be down for some time. Hope had charged and he'd decided he could wait, dropping the meat. It wasn't like he needed to eat. It had just smelled so good.

He stared at Grace, admiring the dragon she'd become. Black as night scales, like him. They gleamed, tips rainbow tones. Like oil dropped in water. Gorgeous.

Grace was tiny. Tinier than he and Hark. Similar in size to his brother's mates. Seeing the difference, he wondered if the diseases and weapons humans used in centuries past changed their basic structure. Perhaps all mates that started as humans would be this size.

He shrugged. It didn't matter. Maybe smaller dragons would allow more dragons to be born. The thought perked up his dragon. Shifting, he lumbered toward his mate.

Her growl stopped him in his tracks.

Rog stepped back until she relaxed once again.

Her eyes stayed glued to him while she continued to daintily devour the carcasses in front of her.

He settled down, laying in the grass. He noticed Hark landing next to him.

Are you done? Rog needed to make sure his mate had plenty.

I think so. There are four more piles of meat. Enough for all of us. Hark plopped down, lying next to him.

Good.

Yes. And plenty of game and cattle here. We didn't even make a dent in the numbers.

It would make a wonderful home. Rog's heart warmed, thinking of it.

Yes, I think so too. Hark nodded. *If the humans don't wake up inside.*

Rog didn't really want to think about that. If they did, there might not be room for them. He eyed the mountains surrounding them. Of course, they could find more caves or another mine in the area to occupy. Share this valley with the humans if they woke. If they didn't try to kill them.

These humans had knowledge of the technology lost to the new world. The rooms they'd sealed were proof of that. It might not be safe. Rog had no desire to lose his mate or any of their offspring to the hatred humans instinctively carried for anyone different than them.

He hoped that whatever they did in the cryonics room didn't bear fruit. Shaking his head, Rog decided to face that if the time came. Grace deserved all of his attention.

The pile of food in front of her was gone. Her snout lifted in the air, scenting. She stood, following her nose. Finding another pile, she circled it protectively, growling. Letting the males know this was hers. Ensuring they wouldn't approach, she ate. Slower this time, but still steadily making her way through the pile.

Rog gazed at her indulgently.

For all her diminutive size, Grace ate enough for a dragon his size. She was beautiful. Perfect.

He watched her eating slow.

A burp appeared to startle her, her wings ruffling at the noise. She sighed, resting her head on a forearm.

A chuckle from his right caught his attention. Zeru. His blue dragon watching the female's moves. "She appears to be done."

"For now." Indra, his dragon a mix of brown and green, a camouflage of colors, spoke. "I will touch nothing until she gives us permission."

"Definitely. Rog here," Hark nodded toward him, "nearly got attacked by a newly turned dragoness. He decided she wouldn't miss a bite." He laughed. "Big mistake."

Rog grinned, teeth wide. "I won't make that mistake again." He turned to Indra. "What type of dragon are you?"

"Woodland Earth dragon." Indra looked at him. "We control the paths of rivers and streams. Among other things."

"That would be handy." Rog nodded. "Zeru, you are an air dragon, correct?" His blue coloring and the ability to camouflage to the sky while flying made him pretty certain his guess was correct.

"Yes." Zeru answered. "Are you fire dragons? I thought your species went extinct centuries ago."

"Yes, even before the humans destroyed themselves." Indra hopped a bit closer. "How are you here?"

"We hibernated." Hark nodded toward the mountain range. "Deep inside the volcanoes. Even the ones humans considered inactive."

"Especially the ones humans considered inactive. We woke during the apocalypse and our sire and dam decided we needed to continue to hibernate, let the world settle. We woke again recently. Two of our brothers were called to their mates. Now me to mine."

A snort brought all attention back to Grace. She lay, eyes closed, snoring softly.

Rog stood. "Look at her." She was so beautiful. He approached her, circling her smaller body with his.

She blinked, snuggled closer to him, and dozed off again.

His heart filled. Satisfied his mate was happy. "I think it's safe to eat."

The dragons dispersed. Each landing near a food pile and digging in.

Hark tossed a carcass to him.

They both froze at Grace's stirring. Moving once she stayed asleep.

Rog quickly ate Hark's offering. *Thank you.*

No problem.

His stomach could stand another bite, but Rog contentedly wrapped around Grace. It wasn't everyday he had a new mate.

Another one of the deceased beasts landed in front of him, followed by a second. "Thanks." Indra and Zeru couldn't speak telepathically with him. Unless they stayed, they never would.

They answered in grunts, still chewing.

Gobbling up the rest of the food in front of him, Rog burped, and curled around Grace. Yawning, Rog settled his head over his mate's neck. Full belly, warm sun, and the delightful feel of his mate cuddled into him were perfect ingredients to a nap.

***

Grace jumped, startled. A clang of metal on metal woke her. She cried out, but instead it came out as a roar. Looking down, she realized the transition worked. Black scales coated a mean looking claw with wicked looking talons. She swung her head around. Wings. She wiggled her butt and watched her tail swing.

A snort had her craning her head back.

Rog's amused eyes stared back.

Grace smiled, loving the indulgent look in his eyes. "How… Oh wow! I can talk in this form." She gazed around, heat suffusing her face, seeing four male dragons watching her. She backed up, stopping only when she pressed against Rog. "How do I change back?"

"Think about being human. Something you'd only do in that form. Eventually it will be easy." Rog's words rumbled from his chest.

Grace felt the vibrations through her side where she pressed against him. Just the feel of him next to her sent her brain skittering down thoughts of being wrapped around him.

Arms slid, encircling her. Moving her until she pressed against him.

Looking up, Grace grinned. His human face loomed above hers. His hard body sent tingles through her. "I did it."

Then she became aware of dragon roars, then hooting. She wasn't the only who'd shifted. Looking down, Grace realized she stood in the nude. Where they could all see her. It felt weird. She shouldn't care, but the heat from a blush rose from her toes to her face.

"You did." The pride in Rog's voice made her giddy.

Taking a deep breath, Grace realized Rog spun her so she wasn't on display. With her important bits plastered against Rog, they could only see her back end. But still. Peeking around his arm, the gazes of the other men stared back.

She ducked her head, burying her face against Rog's chest. "Can't you make them go away?"

"I could, but someone still needs to grab your clothes and bring them over." Rog's chin rubbed her hair. "Unless you wanted to do it yourself."

The thought of racing around naked, not knowing who could see her at any given moment appalled her. The guys didn't seem to care that their junk hung out for the world to see, but she wasn't that girl. Until today, only Rog and her mother had seen her naked. She ignored that fact the men around her also had, since it had been almost a compulsion due to the pheromones. It would never happen again, so no need to show off her goods.

"No. I would appreciate someone gathering them. Then if they would turn around while I dressed, that would be great." Grace practically whispered it. Even her ears burned. Until she clothed herself, she was sure she'd be red.

Even if the breeze cooled her down a bit, it wasn't enough.

"Hark, grab Grace's clothes, would you?" Rog hollered, not even turning around.

"Sure thing."

"What was the noise I heard? Sounded like metal hitting metal." Grace looked around. "Where did it come from?"

Rog shrugged. "It must have been one of the other dragons."

"Not I." A deep voice rolled across her ears. "Nor Zeru. We were hunting after our nap."

She didn't bother to look up. She knew that voice belonged to the earth dragon.

"Hark? Did you make that noise?" Rog looked toward his brother.

"No." Hark shoved her clothes in her arms. "Get dressed."

Both brothers turned toward the door in the mountainside.

"Do you think?" Hark ran his hand through his hair.

"What else could it be?" Rog glared at the door.

"Trouble?" Zeru looked from them to where they were staring.

Grace scrambled to get her clothes on. Could the ancients in the room have woken up? She had to see.

"We found people in individual coffins in some sort of liquid. There were directions on one of them, so we followed it."

"Coffins?" Indra came over, glancing at Grace and looking away.

She couldn't help but feel a bit of outrage at his dismissal. "They were in a room marked cryonics."

"Oh." Zeru hissed out. "Frozen. They put themselves into a freezing sleep hoping they would be woken up once the war was over. I heard rumors of humans doing this. I don't know who they thought would wake them. I don't think they counted on the devastation, or the loss of so many people." He shook his head. "I never heard of a success. Just humans being froze."

"It is probably some former government lab." Indra snorted. "It's probably filled with the type of humans that caused the destruction. The government came and went from this area."

"We did seal up a couple of rooms. One said weapons development and the other something about diseases."

"Sealed how?" Indra asked. "If they are part of the former government, they can't be trusted."

"We used our dragon fire. Melded the door back into becoming one with the wall." Rog slid an arm around Grace, tugging her against his side. "If necessary, we can destroy everything in those rooms. Burn it all."

Like he couldn't not touch her. Her heartbeat thumped. Loud enough Grace was surprised Rog couldn't hear it. Her arm snaked around his waist. Her mind kept drifting to him, despite the conversation.

Indra shrugged. "Maybe it will keep them out."

"How do you know all this?" Hark looked him in the eye. "Hearsay?"

"No. I've been around since before what the humans call the apocalypse. It was easy enough to camouflage. Earth dragons tended to congregate in what used to be National Parks. We could blend in easily. And we held down jobs. Usually in the forestry department."

"So, you lived when there were airplanes and automobiles?" She couldn't help the fascination in her voice. Those seemed like a fairy tale. To know someone who had actually seen them astounded her.

Rog's arm tightened around her. His glower sent spirals of heat to her belly. He was jealous!

She smiled at him. Only Rog sent tingles through her body and tripped her heart at every turn. Standing on her toes, she tugged his head closer, whispered. "I love you." Then nipped his ear.

A purr. Do dragons purr she wondered? A purr rumbled from his chest. The gleam in his eye making her body sing.

It was good to be alive.

CHAPTER TWELVE

He was drowning in her eyes. A loud clang whipped his head around. "We need to see what is making that noise."

Hark rumbled next to him. "Nothing good I fear."

The dragons around him, nodded.

"Count on me. I've enjoyed the world with most of the humans gone. I have no desire to watch them throw it away again." Indra stared where the noise emanated from.

"And possibly us with it. I stand with you also." Zeru stood by Hark, staring at the semi blocked tunnel.

They were all staring, no one taking the first step.

"I thought the humans were all gone from here." Indra didn't look away from the tunnel. "The human government created this area filled with animals. Then left. I thought they left. No one has ever come here until you."

"Were you the one taking care of the animals?" Grace asked.

Indra nodded.

Rog's stomach tightened. He took a deep breath. Then with his arm around Grace, headed slowly toward the noise.

The sound rang again. Then again, until the rhythmic sound continued at a steady pace. Who knows what sight would greet them? He stood taller, straightening his shoulders. They might as well find out now.

"Let's check it out." Taking a deep breath, Rog headed toward the tunnel and the door leading back into the facility.

Grace's hand slipped into his.

He couldn't stop his smile. Glancing down at her, she looked nervous. She gnawed at her bottom lip, worrying it. His body warmed, he wanted to be the one teasing her mouth.

Another clang brought his attention back. Indra and Zeru hadn't been inside. It would be up to Rog and Hark to take the lead. Though it sounded like they had been present before and after the apocalypse so maybe they had insight he and his brother wouldn't.

Entering, the noise obviously came from the cryonics room. Rog exchanged glances with Hark. Slowly they approached the door. He opened it, sliding into the room in front of all of them. Any issues, Rog would face them before his mate was involved.

He sagged against the door. Relieved, he looked at the container they'd followed the instructions on. "Hark, I need your help."

He strode forward, examining it. The fluid had drained. The man inside blinked, a panicked look on his face. The noise, the continuous clang was the lid, rising inches and dropping back down. Again and again.

"Help." The muffled voice broke up. A cough from the man inside.

"We'll help." He went to one side.

Hark went to the other.

The lid clanged down and began to lift again.

"Now, grab it and lift." Rog's arms strained. The pressure of the machine reversed, trying to press down again. "Lift."

Indra and Zeru joined them, lifting. The metal groaned, creaked then snapped.

They tossed the lid behind the container.

The man reached up, pulling out a small tube from his mouth. He coughed, gagging with its withdrawal. He took a deep breath and with trembling hands, hit a couple of buttons. Restraints, almost unseen, retracted. The man sagged back. Relief in every line of his body.

"Who are you?" Grace peeked around Rog's arm.

Rog stiffened. He'd prefer to keep her from having any contact with the man, but obviously that wasn't going to happen. Not if the warm hand gripping his forearm and Grace's curious face were any indication.

"Steven Phillip. Doctor Stephen Phillip." He looked at all of them. "Do you have any water?"

"I'll get it." Grace skipped out the door.

"Follow her." Rog nodded at Zeru. "Keep her safe." He didn't know if this man was the only one around.

"Why are you in that?" Hark gestured at the container. "Did you really freeze yourself?"

"Who are you people? Where are the assistants that are supposed to wake us?" The man sat up. His gray hair plastered to his skin from the mix of chemicals he'd previously floated in. His pale skin looked like it needed sunlight desperately.

Rog shrugged. "There is no one else here. We found this place and started to explore. Your container had directions, so we followed them."

"How long have you been here?" Indra asked him.

"How should I know? What year is it?" The man ran his hands through his hair, grimacing. "Can you help me out of here?"

Rog nodded. He held out a hand, helping him stand.

The man pressed a button inside the container, cursed and kicked the side.

Rog frowned, watching him. "Take my hand."

Hark grabbed the other hand and they assisted him out.

Rog released his hand, rubbing it against his pants. The man's hands were covered in some type of film, slightly sticky. It must be from the liquid previously surrounding him. A whiff of him hurt his nose. The acrid metallic scent wafting with each move. His dragon shrunk away, burying his nose.

"I don't know the year." Hark stepped back, his nose wrinkling.

He must have found the man as offensive as Rog did.

Grace opened the door, a glass of water in her hand. "Here you go." She handed the man the glass and backed away. "Wow. You stink. I think you should wash up."

Steven's expression looked startled. He lifted the glass and downed the contents. He sniffed his arm. He nodded. "A shower would be nice." He handed the glass back to Grace.

"I'll head to my quarters and wash up. You are more than welcome to wait in my living room while I get ready."

Steven walked hesitantly out of the room. The door swinging shut behind him.

"I'd never heard of cryonics working before." Indra poked inside the container. "This pod appears to have malfunctioned." He stood up, looking around the room. "I wonder if any of the other humans are viable."

"I thought only corpses were frozen, but I don't smell death on the man who just left." Zeru sniffed. "But it's hard to tell."

"Maybe we should follow him?" Hark headed toward the door. "I don't trust him."

"You don't know him." Grace piped up.

"Exactly." Rog nodded at Hark. "Excellent idea."

The other dragons grunted. They all turned and headed out the door. Rog grabbed Grace's hand. Her smooth skin felt right, surrounded by his. The spice of her arousal hit his nose. He misstepped, narrowly missing the door frame. His dragon chortled.

Grace's giggle lifted the worry the awakening of Steven Phillip brought.

Grinning, Rog hugged her to him. "Let's go see what we can find out from Doctor Steven Phillips, shall we?"

***

Grace wrapped her fingers tighter around Rog's. She couldn't contain her giggles. He'd just about ran headfirst into the door, too busy watching her. She'd never thought of herself being able to turn heads, but Rog was proving her wrong.

Her heart was light, joy bubbling through her veins. In addition, the voice inside her sang and chirped with happiness. Mate, mate, mate. She rubbed against her insides, fluttering her wings and wagging her tail to get Rog's attention. From the gleam in his eye, her dragon succeeded.

She wasn't too worried about the man they'd brought back to life. After all, he was only human. Her dragon preened inside her. Something she no longer was. Grace couldn't help the thrill that ran through her.

"Sounds good to me." She couldn't help herself. Grace hugged Rog's arm to her, getting as close as she could.

They trailed the rest of the men, following the stink left behind by the doctor.

Grace wondered what they would learn from him. They entered the first living quarters closest to the cryonics room. Water was running from the bathroom.

Hark lounged on one of the chairs.

Indra was poking around in cabinets and Zeru sat on a loveseat.

Grace tugged Rog over to the sofa, sitting down and snuggling into his side.

"Do you think we'll be able to wake all of the people in the pods?" Indra leaned against the counter in the kitchen area.

"Do we have to?" Zeru put his feet on a table in front of him. "I don't know that I like bringing more humans back."

"We need to find out why they were frozen." Rog looked toward the bathroom door. "Can you tell us, Doctor Steven?"

Grace hadn't realized the shower ended.

The doctor stood in the door. Dressed and rubbing his hair with a towel. "Yes." He moved further into the room, sitting down in a chair and tossing the towel toward the bathroom.

Grace watched it land on the floor. A little machine scurried from the wall, picking it up. Her jaw dropped. The machine took it into the bathroom, then moved back, closing itself back in the wall.

"We were part of a scientific community. When the news came of the attack on the US, we headed here. One group was to be frozen here, one in another location and a third group was split and would monitor us both."

"So, you've been frozen since the apocalypse?" Her voice rose. Grace could hardly believe it. "Why?"

"So we can restore order after the attack." Steven leaned forward. "So, how many years have passed? One, two years? What year is it?"

Grace's breath caught. She looked around the room, not sure what to say.

Zeru and Indra looked as shocked as she did.

Rog laughed. "Try two hundred."

"Or maybe three." Hark chimed in, a smirk on his lips.

Grace watched disbelief fill the doctor's face. She'd bet Rog and Hark thought he was joking. "Are any of you contaminated or carry any diseases from the apocalypse?"

"Of course not. We were frozen once the first missile hit." Steven snorted. "I wouldn't call an attack on the US an apocalypse."

Really. Rog snorted.

Grace shook her head. "If you were around when it hit, then you could be contaminated. You could carry one of those diseases." She pressed her lips together. Grace leaned into Rog. "What if he has a disease? We won't know until it spreads."

"Chances are if he's really been frozen for so long any diseases are dead." Indra shrugged. "We can't know for sure, but not many diseases would last so long."

"Even if they were frozen with him?" Zeru leaned forward. "Didn't humans used to freeze people to try to find cures? Which means they could be frozen and not cured."

"Yes, yes. If I carried any diseases, they would become active when I was unfrozen. But I don't have any. If I did, you would be getting sick already."

"That's not true." Indra added. "Most have an incubation period."

The doctor sniffed. "It doesn't matter. I'm not sick."

"Luckily your diseases never affected us. Only the humans." Rog leaned back, a sly smile on his lips.

"Ha, ha." The doctor seemed a bit humorless. "All right. Be honest. How long have I been frozen?"

Grace leaned forward. She shivered when Rog's hand slid down to her waist. "It has been nine generations since the world was destroyed. Give or take." She shook her head. "I don't know how long you've been frozen. I don't know what you mean by what year is it?"

"I can't have been frozen that long. We should have been awakened after a year." He stood up. "That doesn't make any sense."

"The people assigned to wake you probably died. We found the door to this facility in a mine. It was padlocked from the outside and locked from the inside." Rog inserted.

"Then how did you get in?" The frustration in the doctor's voice was evident.

Hark flexed his arms. "With these. We tore the locks off then pulled the door open." He deflated a bit. "It did take both of us though."

"I need to check on the others." The doctor ran his hands through his hair. "We were never supposed to be frozen more than a few years." He mumbled, leaving the room. "If it has truly been that long, they may not wake up."

Grace sat and watched him leave. No one else moved. What could they do? The possibility the people in the lab would never wake up was sobering. She rubbed her belly. Her stomach suddenly ached. "What should we do?" She turned to Rog.

"I suppose we can go see if he needs help." Rog's arm tightened around her waist.

Her stomach growled. Her cheeks heated at Rog's laugh.

"Then food." Rog nuzzled her neck, sending the hair on her nape to attention.

"Sounds good to me. Let's go." Grace stood up, tugging at Rog's hand.

The men all stood up, nodding.

Grace led the way, Rog's hand held tightly in hers. The men followed. A thrill raced through her. She liked them listening to her, following her. No one listened to her at home.

They stopped at the door to the cryonic room.

"I'll get food." Indra turned, heading outside.

"I'll help." Zeru followed him.

Grace sighed, watching them leave. Even though she only had the hots for Rog, the others were some fine-looking men.

"Hey. Eyes here." Rog turned her head toward him. "I'm your mate."

Grace laughed and tossed her arms around his neck. "And I couldn't have a better one."

Rog grumbled. "Then keep your eyes here, where they belong." He pulled her into him.

Hark rolled his eyes, and went inside the room, ignoring them.

Grace arched, loving the feeling of Rog's hands roaming her body. She shivered at the touch of his hands against her skin. His lips sealed to hers, stealing her breath.

Lifted in the air, pulled against him felt like flying while he moved, sliding into a different doorway. Pressed between the hard wall and Rog's hard body thrilled her.

His hand slid in her pants. His warm fingers sliding easily in her desire.

Her body caught fire. Grace moaned, a shiver escaping her control. Her nape heated. Her heartbeat increased.

"Please." Grace needed more. She wiggled, moving one arm from his neck to shove down her pants. When they were as far as she could get them while still kissing Rog, she started shoving his down. He didn't need to be naked to quench the fire in her veins.

Pressed flat against the wall, held up by the strength of his body, Grace lifted a leg, shook her pants off it and wrapped both legs around his hips.

"Ahh." The deep groan from Rog incited her more.

Flames leapt from his body to hers. Everywhere they touched was afire.

Grace couldn't get enough. Her awkward attempts to ride Rog's cock while he attempted to thrust left her almost in tears.

"Stop. Stop. This isn't working." Rog's hoarse voice froze her.

Not working? He thought they weren't working? Ice filled her veins, creeping toward her heart. He couldn't really mean that.

"Move with my hands. We'll get in rhythm, then it will work better. You're driving my dragon crazy." His voice deepened. "Driving me crazy. I. Need. You." Each word was punctuated by a thrust.

Shock rolled through her with each thrust. Okay. The rhythm wasn't working. Damn, it was now. Tremors raced through her. Her pussy tightened on Rog. Pulling him deeper, squeezing until her body and his trembled and exploded. Heat pulsed inside her. Thank goodness the wall was behind her. Her legs shook, wrapped around Rog.

He slid down, landing on his knees on the floor. "That. Worked." Rog panted between words.

"Yeah." Enough words. Grace's body wasn't responding. She leaned against the wall. Slid to the floor.

Rog leaned against her. His forehead resting against her. A wet kiss hit her nose.

She giggled.

Rog laughed. "I think I died. But I died happy."

"Me too." It was hard to respond. She gulped air, trying to even her breathing. The heat they'd called up dissipated. Now, cold was creeping in. Specifically, her butt. Sitting on the stone floor. Unclothed. "I need my pants on."

"I need your pants on too." Hark laughed. "You two need to come help."

Oh, good lord. She forgot her mind when Rog kissed her, touched her. The man, her man, was lethal. In the most delicious way.

CHAPTER THIRTEEN

Groaning, Rog stood up, yanking his pants up. He held out his hand to help Grace up.

You have the worst timing.

You should be thanking me. The human was going to come looking for you.

Thanks. He really wouldn't have cared but Rog knew Grace would. Humans were hung up on not being naked. Grace wouldn't change her attitude in only a day.

Rog slid a hand down her flank, admiring the curves of her while she tried to get redressed. Pink under her skin followed the path his hand took. He moved closer, hands grasping her hips. Rog leaned down, nipping her ear. "Wish we had more time. Days, weeks with nothing but you and me."

Grace squeaked, then melted against him.

"I'll dress you if I have to." Hark stood behind him, grinning.

Rog winced at Grace's squeal.

She grabbed her pants, hopping to put them on while covering herself from Hark.

Rog couldn't help but chuckle.

All it earned him was a glare.

"For Pete's sake." Hark closed in, grabbed Grace's pants and yanked them up.

"Hark!" Her protest ignored.

Rog looked at Hark. Then both started laughing.

Grace shoved the two of them out of her way, nose flaring.

Her stomps echoed, heading toward the cryonics room.

"Smooth." Rog shook his head, stifling his laughter.

Hark flashed him a grin. "She'll forgive me. Eventually."

Rog chuckled and followed Grace. His brother's footsteps mirroring his.

Swinging open the door, his eyes sought Grace.

She prowled the room, peering into the capsules, trailing her fingers along the glass covering them. Her dark hair tumbled down just past her shoulders.

Her mussed look heating his blood. She looked delectable. Fire licked along his veins. Ignoring the human, Rog stalked her way. His hands slid around her waist.

Grace jumped.

Rog sniggered, tightened his grip.

"We need to wake these people up." The human dragged his attention away from Grace.

Rog growled. "Why?"

Steven sputtered. "Why? Because we need to."

Rog released Grace and spun toward Steven. "I see no need to. Humans are what led to the apocalypse. We've been so much better since humans almost wiped themselves from the world."

"Ha ha. You're human too." He walked over to Rog, pointing his finger in his face. "You don't have the right to decide. I'm in charge of this facility. I answer to the US government. Not some random stranger."

Rog's eyes narrowed, his fury building. Growling, Rog shifted, sending a burst of flame to the floor. His anger eased seeing Steven pale and jump back. Rog shifted back. "No, I'm not human. And neither are any of us here. Except you."

"Wha…how…who…what are you?" The quaver in Steven's voice sent a sense of satisfaction through Rog.

"We are the ones who benefitted from your human mistakes." Rog glared at the man.

"You should know there is not a government." Grace slid her arms around Rog. "There hasn't been since most of the people died."

Zeru and Indra strode in.

"Food is outside by the fire." Zeru looked from Rog to Steven.

Steven shook his head. "This doesn't make sense. We were prepared for any eventuality." He grabbed a stool from a monitoring station, plopping down. "How did you people evolve from this?"

Zeru raised a brow. "You people? We have always been here. You people are the ones who ruined what you built. Lucky for us."

Indra nodded. "We were here before your technology came into play. We helped the few that remained survive. And we are still here. Your human diseases did not affect us."

"Some of us hibernated." Hark added.

"And some of us have always been here." Zeru leaned against the door. "Living in silence."

"Watching and trying to minimize the damage humans did to the world." Indra wandered around, looking at the still figures encased in glass. He stopped at one. Looked back at the group. "Who is this?"

"My daughter." He pointed to the next container. "That's my son."

"Is that why you want to wake them all up?" Rog grabbed Grace's arms, placing her in front of him. Her nearness sent his blood surging. Since his outburst he no longer wore his clothes. Placing her in front of him just kept his reaction to her hidden.

Grace's rubbed subtly against him, proving she knew.

His hands tightened on her arms. He pressed against her, shifting his groin. He stifled a groan.

Really? Hark sent him a smirk.

Just wait until you find your mate.

Hark turned and left, coming back and tossing a pair of pants toward him.

Rog grabbed them, catching them before they hit Grace in the face. *Asshole.* He pulled them on, then embraced his mate again.

Steven ran his hands through his hair. He leaned forward, resting his elbows on his knees and his head in his hands. His knuckles turned white, massaging his scalp. "I don't know what to do? How can I believe you?"

Grace turned to look at Rog. "We could take him to my town. He can see for himself."

Rog wondered if that would be enough. He hadn't been there, so couldn't say for sure. "Would it be better to go in the morning?"

Grace shrugged. "Are we going to fly there? Or walk?"

"Fly of course." Zeru added. "I always fly."

"You have a plane?" Steven sat up. "Where do you keep it?"

"No, no planes. No cars, nothing that runs on fossil fuel." Indra added.

"Then how…" Steven trailed off. "Dragons." He swallowed. "Not sure I can do that."

"You've no choice." Rog told him. "We don't want to lose a whole day or more walking."

"Is she human?" Steven pointed at Grace. "She mentioned a town, but I thought you were all dragons."

"I was recently turned. I was human until yesterday." Grace preened.

Rog rubbed his chin on her head. "She's my mate." He couldn't stop the pride in his voice. The confidence Grace exuded intoxicated him.

Steven stared. Eyes wide. His mouth opened and closed.

"We've always been able to turn humans. From the lack of dragons, we don't just willy nilly go out and do it." Rog sighed. "If we did, you would have known about dragons a long time ago."

"We only change our mates. If you're not a dragon's mate, you're safe." Hark added.

"It only works with certain chemicals in our system. They won't active until we meet our mate." Indra added.

Rog glanced at Indra, staring into the pod containing the doctor's daughter. He hadn't seen Indra move since he first glanced in. Rog glanced from the doctor to Indra. This was going to be fun. He'd bet Indra's mate was sealed in that pod.

Grace snuggled closer to him.

His mind snapped from Indra to her. Nothing captured his attention more than his mate. Her soft skin and laughing eyes captivated him. "You want to take him there?"

"I guess. He can see we're not lying then." She frowned.

He just wanted to smooth it away.

"What if he is contagious?" Grace stared at Steven. "He could wipe out the whole town."

"Maybe we should start by introducing him to Lavinia." Hark spat her name out.

Rog couldn't help but laugh. If they were to infect anyone, she'd be the one they'd choose. But he didn't think it would be an issue. Nor did he want knowledge of dragons to fall into the wrong hands. Lavinia was definitely the wrong hands.

"He doesn't appear sick. I don't think he is. The chemicals he was frozen in should have killed any disease." Rog ran a hand down her cheek. So damn soft.

"He's correct. We were scanned before we were frozen and any anomalies treated. None of us carry any disease." Steven looked around. "I'd like to try to wake everyone before we go."

Rog shook his head. "No. Just in case something goes wrong, someone should be here."

"It takes around twelve hours. We will be gone that long?" Steven stood up, walked over to the pod his children were in. He didn't seem to notice Indra's fixation. "I'd like to try to wake them up."

"Maybe we can wake a couple at a time?" Indra spoke, his attention not wavering.

Rog looked at Hark. Grace warmed his side, his heart in her hands. How could he deny Indra the same opportunity?

Indra deserves the opportunity to meet his mate. Rog hugged Grace tighter to him.

What? Hark looked at Indra, a smirk rising to his lips. *Oh, yes indeed, though the good doctor may not be happy.*

I don't think making him happy is on any of our radar. Rog grinned. *If he doesn't like it, we'll just introduce him to your nemesis.*

Hark's bark of laughter turned all eyes to him. *Yes, we could. If we could trust him. Which I'm not too sure of.*

Me either. But once Indra changes his daughter it would be in his best interests to keep quiet.

***

She knew they were talking to each other. Both Rog and Hark had that look upon their faces. Seeing them look over to Indra, then snicker, she was missing something. Grace wondered if she would ever learn to talk mind to mind.

"Why don't we start the process with the doctor's family?" Grace wiggled out of Rog's arms. She headed over to the doctor and Indra. "We will have time to go to my town and return before they are awake. Especially if we fly."

Both Indra and the doctor nodded.

Zeru harrumphed. "I'm going to eat first."

The gurgle from her stomach made her choice. "I'm hungry too." She headed to the door. She saw Rog and Hark follow her. From the corner of her eye she saw Indra look down into the pod, then follow slowly. The doctor shrugged and followed him.

The smell of roasting meat hit her nose. Her belly cramped. Her vision changed, startling her. "Rog." What on earth?

"It's okay. Hunger can bring on the dragon, especially when you're newly learning to shift." Rog entwined his hand with hers. "You'll learn to control it."

"Just think human." Zeru tossed over his shoulder.

Grace rolled her eyes. Think human and that should do it. Right. She thought about kicking his butt. Foot to the keister. Her vision shifted back. Surprisingly, that did it. Huh. "Thanks."

Zeru looked at her and grinned. Like he read her mind. He stripped, practically daring her to look away.

Rog grunted, stepping in front of her and obscuring her view.

Grace giggled, sliding her arms around his waist. "You know you're the only one I want."

"Yeah, but you don't have to look either." His disgruntled tone melted her heart.

"Next time I'll look away." Grace squeezed Rog tight, enjoying his hard muscles against her softer form. "I don't really want to see him naked anyway. It just felt like a dare."

"Good." Rog sniffed, puffing out his chest. "I'm better looking."

She couldn't stop her smile. He wore his jealously proudly. "Definitely." Grace stepped back, sliding her arms from around his waist. "Now feed me. I'm hungry enough to go dragon."

Hark laughed. "Here you go." He tore off a hunk of meat from the meat roasting on the fire, sliding it on a flat rock. He winked. "We can't have that happen, now can we?"

Grace saw Zeru had shifted. His blue dragon munching on a carcass.

Indra lingered near the door. He blended well with the terrain. His camouflage automatic once he'd shifted. The doctor stood near the fire, looking appalled. His gaze swung from the cow over the pit to the meat being served on a rock.

"Sorry, doc. This is all we have." Hark handed him a piece on a rock.

The doctor gingerly took it. "Don't you have plates and silverware? And must you tear it off with your hands?"

"Not exactly using my hands." Hark lifted his hand. It was covered in dragon scales and his talons sliced the meat off. "I don't normally carry around plates and silverware. They can get heavy flying."

Rog whispered in my ear. His breath sending a shiver down my spine. "We have utensils and plates. We're not heathens."

Grace chocked on a laugh. "Then why the show?"

Rog shrugged. "Because it's fun?" He looked around. "Plus, we don't have enough for more than ourselves. And it's in the living quarters we were in."

"Makes sense." Grace pulled a piece of the sizzling meat from her makeshift plate, dropping it in her mouth. She moaned. Juicy and perfectly cooked. Of course, her dragon evidently preferred it a bit bloodier than she was used to, but the meat melted in her mouth.

Dropping to the ground to sit, Grace quickly ate. "More, please?"

Rog grabbed her plate, cutting off more of the roast and handing it to her. He sat down beside her. His plate refilled also.

Grace devoured a couple of servings.

Rog outpacing her easily. Even in human form he consumed more than most men.

Hark, Zeru, and Indra ate a couple of cows each.

The doctor stared at them. An expression of amazement on his face. He ate slowly, watching their every move.

Grace had no desire to change. She didn't plan on prancing around naked when she'd have to change back to get back into the facility. She never had a lot of clothes. When she headed out to the mountains in the first place, she'd only brought one change with.

"Are we really going to have time to go to my town today?" Grace lay back, looking into the sky. "It's already afternoon. Wouldn't it be better to go in the morning?"

"We could start the process of waking my family. Then they'd be able to go with us." The doctor coughed. "That is, if that is okay."

"Sounds like a plan." Indra shifted back. He pulled on his pants, covering himself.

Grace was beginning to think he was as obsessed as the doctor. She leaned against Rog. "Is there something going on? Indra seems determined to have the doctor's family wake up."

Rog chuckled and whispered in her ear. "I'm pretty sure the doctor's daughter is Indra's mate."

Grace gasped, then smothered it. "Oh wow. He can really tell?"

"Yes. It's a draw. I felt you and headed this way." Rog chucked me under the chin, a shit eating smirk on his face. "Aren't you glad I did?"

Grace's cheeks heated. "You've been useful."

"Let's start the process then. We still have time to go into town, especially since we're flying." Hark walked over to them. "It didn't take us long and we still have plenty of time."

Grace shrugged, looking at Rog. "What do you think?" She still wasn't sure they wouldn't be a hazard to her family. But why not give them chance?

"Fine by me." Rog stood, pulling Grace up. He wrapped an arm in hers, escorting her back toward the cryonics room.

"I think there are enough humans. Why will no one listen to me?" Zeru grumped. He followed everyone inside. "Fine, what's two more?"

Grace held her laugh back. She couldn't figure out if Zeru was just grumpy or didn't care for humans. He'd been perfectly agreeable to her. Indra just seemed intense. Perhaps because he was so old.

They entered the room to find the doctor directing Indra and Hark in what to do. Only minutes passed and they moved on to the next figure.

Rog's arm rested on her shoulders, keeping her next to him. Zeru wandered the room, peering into other pods.

"Done. All we can do is wait." The doctor stood back, arms on his hips. "Hopefully this works."

"Into town then. Grace can you grab your backpack?" Rog removed his arm, patting her on the butt.

She glared at him, then left the room. She'd grab it, only because she wanted to. Grace trotted down the hallway. Her steps echoed down the corridor. She regretted taking the first room they'd come to. It meant she had to trot all the way back. Then go back to the cryo room and back this way to leave again.

She skidded to a stop. They'd be passing this way again. Maybe. But if they were flying, they might be flying from the valley. Looking back and forth, Grace sighed and continued. She'd grab it and headed back.

Flying. A grin popped on her face. Flying! She'd be flying too. Grace sped back to the room, eager to leave.

No one was talking. Rog straightened up at her return, striding to greet her.

Indra still stared into the pod. All his attention wrapped up.

Hark and Zeru were wandering the room, poking into cabinets and peering into the pods.

The doctor busy monitoring the progress on the pods.

"Are we going?" Grace lifted her lips for a kiss from Rog. "Do I get to fly, too?"

"Do you want to?" Rog slid his arm around her waist. "You don't know how, yet."

"It's easy to learn isn't it?" Grace really wanted it to be easy.

"Sure. I'll teach you to fly. Just like Rog taught our brother's mate Hope to fly." Hark grinned, heading over to them.

"No." Rog shook his head.

"You know it's the easiest way."

"No. Grace will pick it up easy enough." Rog turned her, heading out the door. He shouted over his shoulder. "Gonna teach Grace to fly. Come out when you're ready."

Hark followed. Zeru close behind. Only the doctor and Indra remained behind. Indra waved a hand, indicating he heard. The doctor didn't bother.

Grace hurried out to the pasture, bursting out the door into the sunshine. She quickly stripped and thought about being a dragon. Her vision shifted. Looking down, Grace saw her scales, feet and talons. She pranced in place, flapping her wings and ready to fly.

Rog picked up her clothes and put them in her backpack. He pulled off his and added them in there. He tossed it to Hark who stripped, added his clothes and shifted. Hark jumped, pumped his wings and grabbed Grace, pulling her into the sky.

She shrieked, wilding pumping her wings. She could barely make out anything below. A small speck speeding toward her. Rog. It had to be. Grace relaxed, just a bit.

Hark opened his talons, letting her go.

Her eyes widened. Her heart thumped, blood racing. Flapping her wings, her mind frozen with fright, Grace plummeted down. Spiraling, she extended her wings, too scared to move. A breeze lifted her, caught in her wings. A cross breeze buffeted her, sinking her down again.

Grace roared. She didn't want to die. A body slid under hers, stabilizing her. She grabbed on with all her claws.

Grace, sweetheart, let go. I'm under you. I won't let you fall. Rog shrugged, trying to get her to loosen her grip.

He dropped me!

I've got you. C'mon, loosen your grip. Extend your wings. Feel the air around them. You can do it. Rog rolled his shoulders, forcing her to let go, just a bit.

Grace loosened her hold. She wasn't letting go entirely. She didn't want to plummet to her death. She stretched out her wings, feeling the currents. She adjusted, letting the air carry her body forward. She wobbled at a cross current. Tilting her wings, she stayed steady.

Exhilaration curled inside her. She couldn't stop her grin. Slowly she released Rog, trusting him to catch her. Flapping her wings to see if she could go faster.

Good girl. The satisfaction in his tone, wasn't lost on her.

Grace trumpeted her excitement to the sky.

Try adjusting your altitude. We need to circle back around and land. Rog nudged her, tilting his head back to the valley.

Grace pouted. She wanted to continue. With Rog's example, she followed him. Turning and descending presented only minor problems. She corrected the issues with tiny shifts of her wings. Landing and takeoff were going to be her issues.

Below, Rog shadowed her. On the ground Zeru and Indra watched her. Zeru in his dragon. Indra stood talking to the doctor. She didn't see Hark.

A shadow crossed her. Looking up, Hark flew above her.

Her mouth tightened at the grin on his face. She wasn't sure of her flying enough to retaliate right now. But he would find out her opinion of his stunt once she found a suitable revenge. Turning her head away, Grace ignored him.

She concentrated on Rog. Maybe she could do that mind speak stuff again. *How am I supposed to land?*

Watch me. Try to follow what I do. Taking off will be an issue until you have enough wing strength. We'll work on that. Until then, I'll take you up and release you when you're ready. Rog flew around her, nuzzling her neck and returned to his position below her.

She did it. Grace wiggled, happy of both accomplishments. *I'm really flying.*

Yes, you are. Rog's indulgent tone sent a curl of desire through her.

She figured panic helped her fly and talk to Rog. Knowing it was possible, helped.

Watch now.

Grace watched Rog's movements. She knew enough to pay attention to his wings just from this short time learning to fly. Copying his movements, she landed. She ignored the fact she skidded just a bit at the end, tripped over her feet and made a less than perfect landing. She landed after all.

CHAPTER FOURTEEN

Rog watched Grace land. Not the most elegant, but not bad for a first time. *Stay in your dragon. We're going to leave right away.*

Okay.

His mate had mad skills. She could already mind speak with him. None of his brother's mates could even though they'd been dragons longer. Her flying was better than he expected. She even managed to land sort of gracefully.

Grace turned her head, this way and that, checking out her wings.

Rog couldn't stop the smile on his face. She was adorable. It was all he could do to stop his dragon from mounting hers on her maiden flight. With the others watching from below, Rog had no doubt she'd have castrated him.

"Who is carrying the human?" Indra looked at Rog.

Rog frowned. He'd rather not carry the human.

"I will." Zeru sat back, offering his claws as a seat.

Indra ushered Steven over, his hesitation obvious. All the dragons towered over him except Grace.

"Can't I go with that one?" He pointed at Grace.

Rog growled. "No. She's just learning to fly. Unless you want to be dropped." He spread his wings, puffing his chest. Smoke curled from his nostrils.

Steven recoiled, moving closer to Zeru. "Fine. What should I do?" He looked at Indra, clearly unsettled.

"Just grab my leg and sit in my claws. I'll close them around you so you don't fall." Zeru spoke, stretching out his talons again.

Steven gingerly followed his instructions.

Indra stripped, placing his clothes in a bag. He shifted, grabbing it with a talon.

Rog scooped up Grace's backpack. He'd noticed Zeru appeared to have his own bag hooked in a claw. "Ready?"

Everyone nodded.

Rog let the other male dragons leave before him. He smirked, hearing Steven let out a scream in fright. *I have to pick you up. Let me know when to let you go.*

Okay. Her voice was tentative, but he knew she'd be all right.

Rog launched himself in the air, circled back around and grabbed Grace. Good thing she was a tiny thing in her dragon form. Tiny compared to him. Larger than a human, but small for a dragon.

Which way?

Oh. I forgot you don't know where I'm from. Grace shook her head. *It feels like I've known you forever.*

Warmth filled his heart. *Yes, it does. It's a wonderful feeling. Ready for me to let go?*

Grace nodded, smiling.

Her smile lit his soul, filling him with contentment.

This way. She spread her wings, turning to go over the mountain.

The others followed.

Rog didn't hear anymore screaming from Steven. He'd either acclimated or passed out. Rog hoped it was the latter. He'd rather Steven didn't know where Grace lived. If all the people in the pods were unfrozen, they might overwhelm Grace's town. They might carry diseases that hadn't been seen since humans were almost wiped out. Survivors from the apocalypse appeared to be immune to what killed the rest of the population.

Steven and his people probably didn't have that immunity. Some might have, but Rog doubted they all did. Whatever diseases killed off most of the humans could kill off those without the original immunities.

A niggle of worry slipped into his mind. If that were the case, Indra would have to turn his mate sooner rather than later. Rog would have to speak with him. Taking Steven to Grace's community could be a death sentence to him. Or nothing could happen.

They would see.

Rog enjoyed watching Grace gain her confidence flying. Once she built up her wing muscles, she'd be able to launch herself from the ground. Landing? He smiled thinking of her earlier attempt. Landing would take time.

Are you sure this is a good idea? Hark flew closer to the ground, underneath Grace. Occasionally spinning, flying upside down to watch her progress before flipping back over.

Rog didn't believe she'd noticed. *What else can we do?*

He could be carrying something that could sicken all of Grace's town.

Or he could catch something from them. It works both ways. Rog shrugged. He didn't really care either way, but they needed to find out. *Indra's mate's life might depend on it.*

What? Hark's flight stalled, dropping him. He tilted catching a current, rising near Rog. *Indra met his mate? When?*

I believe it is Steven's daughter. Didn't you notice how he hovered over her pod? Rog checked on Grace. She looked to be testing air currents, gliding until she found another in the direction she was aiming for.

No. We were all checking the pods. Hark spun, circling Grace before returning to Rog's side.

Rog grinned.

Grace just missed hitting Hark with her tail. If he was not mistaken, she was aiming for him.

Hark appeared to not even notice.

How did they look? Rog wondered if all the humans were still alive.

Like humans.

Rog sighed. *I meant; do you think we will be able to unfreeze them all?*

Hark shook his head. *No. I could detect the smell of decomposition when I checked some of the seals. Not all of them are viable.*

How many do you think? Rog was glad to hear that. Less humans meant less complications.

Are you sure? Grace chimed in.

Since when can you hear us? Hark flew close to her. He flapped his wings hard, knocking Grace off course.

Rog rolled his eyes at Hark's snicker.

Grace whipped her tail at him, catching him along the belly while she spun to right herself. *Since you dropped me in the air earlier.*

I think panic enabled her to cry out to me. I answered her the same way. Rog puffed out his chest. His mate was a fast leaner.

How much farther to your town? And yes, I'm sure not all the pods are viable. Besides the smell, the liquid is a bit different in color. Probably because of the decomposition. Hark flew around Grace again, circling her.

Rog grimaced. *We'll have to figure out how to dispose of those. And leave my mate alone.* He flew to Hark, head butting him.

Make me. Hark grinned and grappled with him. Soon enough, both brothers were diving and swooping around each other.

Rog heard Grace chuckle, but she left them to it.

***

Boys will be boys.

Rog and Hark wrestled in air. Unlike the boys back home, they looked graceful doing it. Their dragons, both black, sparkled in the sun, moving swifter than Grace ever imagined.

Watching them, she almost missed the town below.

We're here. Talking mind to mind sure beat trying to yell to get their attention.

Both Rog and Hark lifted their heads, drifting away from further engagement. They circled, looking around.

We need to find a place to land. Far enough away from anyone seeing us, but close enough to get there easily. Rog peered down at the landscape below.

I know just the place. Of course, she did. She'd grown up here. Grace flew to the east of town. Below her a meadow spread out. Most people didn't come here. It was uphill from town, too hard to bring equipment to plow. Occasionally a hunter might come through, but the cattle and domesticated animals made hunting more a hobby than a necessity.

Landing, tripping over her own feet, Grace skidded in the grass. Getting to her feet, she shifted. Curling to cover herself, she waited for Rog to land. Dragons thudded down, shifting once landed.

Rog strode over, handing her clothes to her.

Grace scrambled into them, back turned to the men. Sitting down, she put on her shoes. Once ready, Grace jumped up. "We can head in from here. It's about a thirty-minute walk."

"Why so far?" The doctor, still looking green, asked.

"I don't want to get shot out of the sky." Grace rolled her eyes. Stupid question. She didn't know about dragons until she'd met Rog. If any of the townspeople knew, they'd never said. No need to start a panic if they didn't by dropping out of the sky right in the middle of town.

Grace grabbed Rog's hand and they moved to head to town.

Time passed quickly while they walked. Indra and Zeru questioned the doctor and pressed for information about the freezing process. The doctor went into information detailed enough to make my head spin.

"It would be best if no one mentions the facility in the mountains. Or that you were cryonically frozen, Steven. We don't know what the townspeople will do if they know." Rog's fingers squeezed mine. "I don't think everyone would be as accepting as Grace."

"Some would demand to see it. Some would take what they could carry." Grace shrugged. She knew sharing the information with the wrong people would have the place invaded. Bartering was alive and well in her town. But everyone had a place to sleep and food to eat. Sharing of these were mandatory. Luxuries on the other hand, were up to the individuals.

The town came into view. Grace walked, head held high, down the street toward her family's home. The roads were dirt and stone, ground down over the years. Shops with doors open for business.

Green could be seen around the homes, the fronts decorated with flowers, the backs filled with gardens of every variety. If they walked long enough, they would find the cemetery. The wrought iron fence encasing the dead. The graves and tombs from decades and centuries past.

"Shall we go visit my family?" Grace looked to Rog.

He nodded his head.

"But I want to find out more about the government." Steven interjected. "Who I can contact. And how they want me to proceed."

The men frowned.

Indra shook his head. "Your government, as you remember it, no longer exists."

"I can take you to the library. I'm sure you can find information there." Grace smiled at Steven even though she wanted to shake him. He didn't listen. She didn't understand his insistence at someone else telling him what to do.

"Well, who is in charge here?" He glared at her, backing down when Rog bared his teeth and growled.

"I suppose the sheriff." Grace thought about it. "But only to keep law and order."

"What about the mayor or governor?"

Grace stared at him. "What's that?" The only ones who pretended they were in charge were Lavinia's family. She wasn't about to head there with him.

"Why don't we just see how everything works here?" Indra placed a hand on the doctor's shoulder. "Every town I've visited has run a bit different. Plus, we need to be back when your daughter and son wake up."

Steven took a deep breath and let it out. "I suppose."

"We can come back again. It's not like you're a prisoner." Hark rolled his eyes. "Grace, lead on."

She couldn't help the quick smile. "Let's go see if any of my family are home." She turned to Steven. "I can show you around while we walk."

Linking arms with Rog on one side and the doctor on the other, she pointed out the market, lively at this time of the day. The blacksmith, the herbalist, the doctor's office, the dentist, the veterinarian, the school and library were the main businesses. Others lined the walk, their wares obvious from the items in the windows. It wasn't a huge main street, but everything they needed could pretty much be found or made there.

Grace ignored the eyes following her group. The dropped jaws at the handsome men with her. She saw more than one finger pointed and heads together gossiping.

The doctor's demeanor deflated by the time they turned the corner. They stood in front of the sheriff's office. Alongside it, a courtroom and a hanging tree facing the cemetery.

"That's it?" the doctor's voice low.

Grace bit her lip and nodded. "Do you want to check out the library? They might know more information."

"How do you get power?" He looked at the lights on in various places.

"Oh, that's easy. Solar and wind power. There's a generator that runs from the river, but we only use that in winter." Grace pointed to the roof tops. "See? Every house has a solar panel."

"Let's go find your family." Rog pulled Grace in close. He whispered into her ear. "The natives are getting restless."

"Fine." Grace snuggled in his embrace, then stepped back. "This way." She passed the Sheriff's continued down the road a bit before turning down another road heading back toward town.

Zeru, Hark, and Indra looked curiously around them.

"The homes are well maintained." Zeru leaned down to touch a blooming rose bush.

"It doesn't look like a compound or anything. Nothing fenced in or barricaded like Hope and Faith's home." Hark looked around. "I like it."

A burble of joy bubbled inside Grace. "Thank you. Though I didn't do it. But what are their homes like?" She figured Hope and Faith were their brother's mates, though she wasn't positive.

"Joyless. The whole town they live in has fences around every family compound. They get most of their food from hunting. It makes for a lean life." Rog looked around. "They have one large farm that everyone works on for grain and crops to share."

"If you don't work there, you don't get the grain." Hark added.

"That's crazy. Food is a necessity. No one goes hungry here." Grace waved her arm around. "You can see, every home grows a garden. Everyone either cans or dries food. Any excess is shared in the market." She shook her head. "It makes no sense to have anyone go hungry."

Rog shrugged. "It's just the way their town is. They discourage any strangers from visiting, also."

Grace's heart hurt. Even though she didn't get along with some of the towns people, they would never starve her. Strangers were encouraged to stay, absorbed into the town. "Wow." Hand entwined with Rog's Grace hugged his arm to her.

She stopped, waved at the house in front of her. "Here's my parent's house." She led the way, opening the door. "Mom, Dad. I'm home and have a few visitors."

Grace wiped her feet on the mat at the door and ushered them all in.

A head popped out of a doorway. "Grace?"

"Yeah, Mom."

"Who do you have with you? Why don't you all come into the kitchen?"

Grace led the way. The room was light, windows lining the wall with a door leading out back. The counters were faded, a pale color from years of use. The cabinets were a natural wood, like most of the homes in town. The table was large with lots of mismatched chairs. Her older brothers had been a rowdy bunch and from years of rough housing and breakage, they were replaced individually.

"Have a seat." Grace gestured at the chairs. "Mom, would you like some help?"

"You can grab some cups. Would you gentlemen prefer milk, chicory coffee or beer?"

"Beer, please." The vigorous nods from the men gave Grace an inkling that cow's milk was not a favorite of the dragons.

"I'd take milk if it isn't a problem." The doctor smiled at her mom.

"Oh, no problem."

Grace grabbed a glass and filled it with milk, handing it to the doctor. She placed glasses out for the rest of the men and retrieved the pitcher of beer, filling each glass.

Her mother brought over a pot and poured out a measure into her cup. "Grab milk if you want some." She pointed to the plate on the table. "You men, help yourself to a cookie or a slice of bread if you'd like."

Grace sat down. Pulling the plate toward her, she grabbed a cookie. "Anyone?"

They all shook their heads, so Grace pushed it back into the center of the table. Hark grabbed a slice of bread, moaning after the first bite. Then each man grabbed a slice.

Grace snickered. Each one moaned after the first bite, gobbling it down quickly.

"So, who do you have here?" Her mom looked around the table.

"This is Rog."

He smiled at her mom, leaning over to shake her hand, while his cheeks remained full.

Grace snickered. No one made bread like her mom. She'd had plenty of experience with her children and grandchildren to perfect it.

"This is Hark, Zeru, Indra, and Doctor Steven." Each nodded in turn, all of them occupied with the treats on the table.

"Where did you meet them?" Her mom sipped her coffee.

"Hark and Rog rescued me. I slipped down the side of the mountain and was trapped. I met Zeru and Indra on the other side while we were exploring." Grace prayed the heat creeping around her ears didn't make it to her face. She didn't want to mention it was her everyone was exploring. "Steven was an unexpected visitor." Too say the least.

"How long have you lived here? The town looks well established." The doctor leaned forward. His intense gaze got nothing more than a raised eyebrow from her mom.

"You're definitely not from around here. Our family has been in this home for generations. Our family lived here from before the apocalypse. This town was here already. Back then it was just a small town with a defunct water generator and mill."

A smile ghosted across her mom's lips. "The town had volunteered to be part of a government experiment with solar power. Lucky for us."

The doctor nodded. "What kind of government exists around here? Surely you have some."

Her mom shook her head. "Nope. The sheriff and his deputies. A town charter was made when the country's government failed. It's mostly the commandments from the old bible. They made sense. If we have someone break one of the laws, a jury is convened and a sentence handed down."

"Of course, we have those busybodies that want to tell everyone else what to do." Grace couldn't help the snide tone in her voice. Lavinia and her family came to mind.

"If they break the law, they will face the same consequences as everyone else." Her dad's baritone rang out. "Unpleasant they might be, but they are not above the rest of the town, no matter what they think. Grace, who are all these men?"

Grace cringed, not answering. Luckily her brother Paul started talking.

"Lavinia said her brother is going to force Grace to marry him." Paul slid in past her dad, leaning over to kiss Grace's cheek and then her mom's.

"Oh, that's just talk. He'd never do such a thing." Her mom swallowed the rest of her tea, putting it down forcefully on the table.

"Lavinia didn't think so. She came to make sure Grace knew." Paul grabbed a cookie from the table, crunching it between his teeth.

"No, she came to 'keep me pure'" Grace finger quoted.

Paul snorted, looking at Rog. "Nope, she did come to warn you about him. She doesn't want you to marry her brother. She hates this family."

"Your brother should never have led her on, then left her." Her mother's sharp tone drew Grace's attention back to her. "She hurts from his behavior, and rightly so."

"My brother wouldn't do such a thing." Paul grimaced. "And besides she shouldn't be taking it out on Grace. You know this and didn't do a damn thing about it." Paul argued. "Who knows where Peter's at. No one ever saw him again. I'm sure something happened to him. It's not his fault he left Lavinia."

"You don't know everything." Her mother stood, the chair screeching on the floor.

"Lois, leave it be." Her father frowned. "It's old news, let it lay."

"Maybe it's time the truth came out." Her mother crossed her arms, facing a rapt audience.

"You mean, Lavinia could have been my sister in law?" Grace wrinkled her nose. She couldn't imagine a sourpuss like her in the family.

"No." Lois swallowed. Her face determined.

"Let it be." Her dad grabbed her arm. "Don't. It's not your secret to tell."

"No, Grace should know." She pulled her arm free from him. "Lavinia is your mother."

The words from Lois's lips froze Grace. The pit of her stomach roiled. She sat there, not knowing what to do. Surely, it was a lie.

"Bullshit." Paul pulled Grace into his arms. "You had Grace, I remember you being big as a house, shocked you were pregnant."

Her mom closed her eyes, opened them. "I was. The baby was stillborn. Lavinia went into labor the same day. Her parents hid the fact she was pregnant, especially since Peter had disappeared. When my baby died, she begged me to take her baby, pretend it was mine. Said she couldn't bear the indignity of having Peter's child when he'd run off. Don't forget how young she was."

Grace could have heard a pin drop. Her heart stuttered. She didn't doubt her mom's story for a bit. Lavinia always hated her. Something inside her soul crumpled. She breathed in sharply, her breath stuttering out of her. Swallowing, she turned to Rog.

Please.

Rog shoved away from the table, yanking her into his arms. *You'll be okay, sweetheart. I've got you.*

CHAPTER FIFTEEN

Rog had no idea why Grace's mom would blurt out the truth about Grace's parents. It made no difference to him.

He just knew his mate was hurting. He tightened his arms around her, tucking her head under his chin, hiding her trembling from the rest of the room.

Her staccato breathing and silent tears soaking his shirt told him how hurt she felt.

He glared at her mother. Not her mother. Her grandmother. That witch, Lavinia was her mother. He didn't see it. Grace was nothing like her. She looked more like her brother Paul. Rog sucked in a breath. Maybe that was the problem.

Rog looked at Paul. "Do you look like your brother?"

Paul rubbed his face and looked at him. "We were twins. So, yeah." He shook his head. "I never guessed Grace was my niece, not my sister." He looked at his parents. "I would have raised her if I'd known."

"Lavinia didn't want anyone to know. That poor girl went through enough." His mother shook her head. "How would it have looked if I gave my baby to you and Mary to raise?"

"Besides, Grace was like having a piece of Peter here." Grace's dad crossed his arms. "I still don't believe Peter ran away. Something had to have happened to him."

"I've told you that for years. Peter's dead. I know it. I've always known it." Paul sighed. "He was crazy about Lavinia. He wouldn't have left her."

"You don't know that." Lois practically screamed. "Stop saying that."

Paul stood up. "I've got to get home." He rested a hand on Grace's head. "Let me know if you need anything."

Grace nodded, still holding on to Rog.

Paul stopped, turned to his father, anger flashing in his eyes. "You gave Walter permission to marry Grace, knowing he was her uncle."

He snorted. "I knew Grace would never say yes. My girl has more sense than that. Plus, he couldn't know Grace was Lavinia's."

Paul shook his head and left.

"Can we just go?" Grace mumbled into Rog's chest.

"Who are these people, Grace?" Her dad, grandfather asked. "I don't like you going off with strange men."

"It's okay." Grace leaned back, looking at him. "Dad, Rog. Rog, Dennis my…" Her voice trailed off. What should she call him now? "Rog won't let anything happen to me. Hark is his brother. And the rest…" What could she say? "Are from the mountains."

"Maybe you should stay here."

Grace shook her head. The pain in her chest took her breath away. "No. I can't. I just can't." She buried her head back in Rog's chest.

"We're leaving now." Rog shook Grace's grandfather's hand. "C'mon, we'll head back to Grace's place." Hark, Zeru, Indra, and even Steven nodded, standing.

"What are you to Grace? You seem much too familiar with her." Dennis growled, not releasing Rog's hand.

"She is my mate." He didn't want to hurt the human, one Grace was obviously fond of, so he didn't rip his hand away. A small tug and Dennis released him.

Grace's head popped up, a smile wreathing her face. "I'm going to marry him."

Dennis sighed, staring at him. "Don't hurt my girl. You'll answer to me if you do."

"I won't."

"Grace, it's for the best. You needed to know." Lois wrung her hands, ignoring the conversation going on around her.

"Let it be. You've done enough damage to our girl." Her dad, for all intents and purposes, kissed her on head. "We still love you, ya know."

Grace nodded and turned to give him a quick hug.

She didn't say anything more, just hurried past her grandmother.

Rog nodded and followed Grace. He kept his hand on her lower back. He would make sure she always knew he was there. At her back. Forever.

Grace headed the way out of the house.

Rog could feel the trembling of her body. He was proud of her. Amidst the emotional turmoil she'd just faced, she hadn't once let her dragon loose. His woman had control. Rog just wasn't sure how much longer she would have it.

He heard the murmurs of the men saying their goodbyes.

Grace stood in front of the house, breathing heavily, hands clenched.

Rog wished he could take it all away.

She stood there. Her face turned toward the sky Grace let out a scream, clenching her hands. Her face red.

Rog let her get it out. She hadn't shifted. After the news she just got, Grace deserved to let her emotions out.

Grace turned toward him. "I want to talk to her."

"Sweetheart, I don't think that's a good idea." Rog rubbed her shoulder. "What good would it do?"

She shook her head. "I don't know."

"We have time." Indra spoke slowly. "Before the others wake up. If she needs to do this."

"Can we go to Paul's? I can ask Paul to get her." Grace sucked in a breath. Her jagged exhale twisted my gut. "I need to."

"What will you even say?" Hark gazed around at the houses surrounding them.

"I don't know." Grace sniffed. "Something."

Rog nodded. "Let's go to Paul's. Lead the way."

Grace's head swiveled, looking up and down the street. She sighed and walked down the block. She stopped and turned into a yard with a small yellow house. She knocked.

A young woman about Grace's age answered the door. A smile lit her face and she enveloped Grace in a hug. "Grace."

Hugging her back, Grace smiled. Finally. "Is Paul home?"

Lucy rolled her eyes. "Yes, but he's in a pissy mood."

Grace laughed, a short sharp sound. "I hear that."

"I'll get him." Lucy dragged Grace into the house. "Dad, Grace wants to see you."

Rog heard grumbling and Paul entered the room. "What do you need, honey?"

"I want to talk to Lavinia. Will you go see if she'll talk to me?" Grace's arms wrapped around her stomach. Her eyes, clear and determined, stared at Paul.

"Are you sure?" At her nod, Paul nodded and left.

Grace glanced out the window, pacing and staring outside.

"So, Grace, who are all these people?" Lucy ogled each of the men.

Rog wrapped his arm around Grace, pulling her in front of him. Her pacing made his dragon antsy. Plus, Lucy's stare made him prefer to hide from her gaze.

Grace glanced from him to Lucy and snickered. "Luc, leave them alone. Rog here," she tapped his arm, "is mine. So, knock it off." She pointed at each of the men in turn. "Hark, Rog's brother. Zeru and Indra are friends. This is Steven."

"Doctor Steven Phillips." Steven bowed over her hand, kissing the knuckles.

Lucy's brows went up and she pulled her hand from his grasp. "Doctor of what?"

"Of Biology." He gave her a smarmy smile.

Rog was hard put not to laugh at Lucy's expression.

"So not a real doctor." Dismissing him, Lucy checked out the rest of them. "What do the rest of you do?"

"I'm a type of forest ranger." Indra stared at the paintings on the walls. "I try to make sure balance is kept in the forest, help anyone lost or injured I come across."

Rog stared at Hark, shrugging. He couldn't really name what they did. "We survive. Hunt, gather, wander."

Hark nodded.

Zeru frowned. "I do the same. I'm not sure there is a name for it."

"Hmm. So, does that mean you'll start wandering too?" Lucy frowned, staring at Grace. "Since you said—Rog is it? —is yours. What does that mean exactly?"

"We'll be getting married." Rog interjected. "We just spoke to Dennis."

Grace colored up. "We haven't talked about wandering. We'll see."

"Don't you think that should be a discussion you need to have?" Lucy gave Grace a bit of a stink eye, similar to his Dam's when he misbehaved. "Before you get married?"

Paul walked back in and slammed the door as he entered. "She won't come here." He glared around the room. "She said she'll meet you at your house tomorrow. Not Mom and Dad's, your place by the river."

Grace growled. "She has to make everything hard." She plopped down on the couch in the living room.

Everyone else stood around. Her reddened eyes, pursed lips and drawn face made Rog want to wrap her up and hide her away from the world. His first impression of Lavinia wasn't good. Her choice to make Grace wait, just another mark against her.

What type of mother treated her daughter like that? Rog growled. Evidently one that never wanted her child. He worried how talking with Lavinia would affect Grace. He sat next to her, needing her touch, needing to touch her and remove anything that could hurt her.

Unfortunately, it wasn't possible to shield her from this.

Rog wondered why her grandmother broke the news the way she did. He shook his head. His heart ached for his mate. Her grandmother wasn't protecting Grace, that was for sure. Her grandfather looked willing to take the secret to the grave.

Rog didn't want to hear the arguments going on in that house tonight. He'd heard the start of the yelling as the door closed behind him when they had left for Paul's, happily moving away. Grace didn't need to hear it either. She'd had enough, learning Lavinia was her biological mother.

***

Grace burrowed into Rog's embrace. Her mind swimming. Her brain just kept repeating Lavinia was her mother, over and over again. She grasped his arms, holding him to her. Her rock.

She didn't know whether to scream or to cry. Her own mother hated her father so much she gave her daughter away. Her stomach twisted in knots. Her chest ached, holding in her emotions. She could hardly bear to think about it, but it was all she could think of.

Why had her mom told her? What purpose did it serve? Did she resent her, having to take care of her all these years? Pretending to be her mom.

"Let's go." Rog's voice raised her eyes to his. "We need to be back anyway."

Grace nodded. He was right. The people would be waking in a few hours. They needed to be there.

Rog stood, pulling her up after him.

"Are you all right?" Paul looked gray. His skin pallid from the truth they'd learned today.

"Yes." Grace nodded. She would be, eventually. "If you see Lavinia, let her know I'll be there."

Paul frowned and nodded. "Take care of her tonight." He shook Rog's hand.

Opening the door, he ushered them out.

Lucy waved. "Don't be a stranger!"

Grace smiled or tried to. She embraced Lucy. "Good night. I'll talk to you when I figure this out."

"Then spill the beans to me." Lucy whispered, letting Grace go.

Grace felt the loss, Lucy's hug bringing memories of growing up together. Hugging to whisper to get their stories straight before they each went home under their parents frowning gazes. "I will, eventually."

Lucy's nod and familiar acceptance put Grace's world back on a bit of an even keel. At least something was familiar.

Even Paul's narrowing eyes at their whispers was familiar.

Her world wouldn't really change very much. Her parents rarely had the energy to deal with her. She wondered if their baby had lived if that would have changed. Somehow, Grace doubted it. They were just too old to have someone young in their house on a full-time basis. Grace was lucky she and Lucy were so close in age.

What made her stomach turn was knowing that the woman who always seemed to hate her was her mother.

"Good night to all you handsome fellows." Lucy fluttered her eye lashes madly. "Don't forget, I'm single."

Grace snorted, not bothering to smother her laugh.

The men, with the exception of the doctor, edged around her, saying their goodbyes.

"Goodnight, my dear." The doctor tried to grab Lucy's hand again, but she instead closed the door on him with a smile on her face.

The chuckles from the others told Grace she wasn't the only one amused by Lucy.

The doctors harrumph just continued the amusement.

"We need to head back." Indra looked at the sun, now close to the edge of the horizon. He began walking toward the other end of town, where they'd come in.

Everyone fell in step behind him.

"I should check on them, make sure nothing is going wrong." The doctor added.

"We can hunt on the way back." Hark rubbed his belly. "I'm hungry."

"There is food in the housing areas." The doctor added. "I can easily make something. If the food containment systems are working."

"You can make dinner for yourself, then." Rog picked up his pace. "The rest of us will hunt. Grace needs to learn."

Grace perked up. Learning something new would take her mind off what she'd just learned. "As a dragon?" The churning in her belly changed to excitement. The hollow pit of what she'd learned didn't leave entirely, but focusing on something else definitely helped.

"I'll take Steven back and join you." Indra didn't seem to even notice the passing buildings. His steps continued, steadily eating up the ground.

The trees approached. The setting sun placed shadows everywhere. Grace thought they'd be able to change closer than the area they'd originally landed. The darkness would hide their dragons. Definitely her, Rog and Hark. Their black scales would blend seamlessly into the night. Even Indra's camouflage green and brown would seem unremarkable. But Grace had no idea how Zeru with his blue scales would blend. As long as the moon wasn't shining brightly, she supposed they would all be hidden.

"Grace, are there any homes out here?" Indra turned to her.

"No." She shook her head.

Indra stripped. All the men did.

Reluctantly Grace pulled off her clothes, keeping her back to them and hiding behind Rog to his amusement.

Rog stuffed the clothing into her backpack.

Indra, Zeru and Hark had already shifted. Rog followed, his scales brushing up against her skin.

Grace shivered, her nipples puckering in the cold. "Move so I can shift." She pushed Rog away to get some room.

His snort at the treatment pulled a grin from her.

"You know I need more room. Unless you want me to prance around naked in front of everyone."

His growl and shuffling backwards gave her his answer.

Grinning, Grace thought about being a dragon. Her belly growled. The thought of a nice fat deer, roasting over the fire set her mouth to salivating. Her sight changed, the trees around her becoming sharper.

Grace looked down at her feet in satisfaction. She'd done it. She shifted. Her talons gleamed in the moon rising in the sky. She clicked them, enjoying the sound. Grace cocked her head. Even the insects stopped humming. The fallow field, surrounded by trees, lay silent.

She wanted to roar into the night. But they were too close to the town. The noise would bring the townsfolk running. It was too big a chance to take.

Claws gripped her, dragging her into the sky.

Darn it. You have to teach me how to fly by myself.

Rog's chuckle her only answer.

Her dragon snorted. The indignity. Falling suddenly, Grace shrieked. She flapped her wings, slowly stopping her fall. Wobbling, she gained in altitude. Glaring at Rog she thought hard at him. *Next time give me a warning.*

Hark's laughter and Rog's smirk told her they heard her loud and clear.

Watch us hunt. Hark arrowed in on a herd bellow. *Aim for the slowest, you'll have a better chance of catching one.*

Rog and Hark tag teamed, keeping the herd running in one direction.

Grace followed, paying attention to the last deer in line. She dove, sinking her talons into the beast. In her periphery she saw Rog and Hark catch a pair each.

Zeru dove in, grabbing a couple also.

Indra, with his burden of the doctor, shifted him to one claw and snagged a deer with the other.

The doctor screamed, blood from the animal smattering in his face. His arms visibly tightening around Indra's leg.

Maybe she should get a second one also. Grasping the deer tightly in her claws so she didn't accidentally drop it, she dove. The wind whistled past her. Opening her jaws, Grace bit down. Her teeth jarred, smashing together when she missed her target. Climbing and diving again, she crowed in victory around the squirming animal in her mouth.

Blood splashed her throat. Grace swallowed it down. Her stomach rumbled in anticipation, the taste on her tongue sending her hunger climbing.

Next to her, Indra dropped down, grabbing another deer in his mouth. He glanced at her and smiled around his still squirming prey.

Now you have to land. Rog laughed. *Once we get over the mountain, drop your prey in the field and try to land. Put your feet out, slowing until you are hovering. You should be able to land without rolling or skidding then.*

Grace nodded. With her mouth full, she couldn't seem to piece the words together to even think them at Rog. But, if she was able to slow, hover and land, why would she need to drop her catch?

Stubbornly, she kept her claws dug into the deer and her teeth firmly in the other. She slowed, watching Hark and Rog. Hovering they released their catches, landing next to them. Grace slowed, backing winging to slow even more, just like them and opened her claws. Her deer thudded on the ground. Tilting her wings, barely moving them, she landed next to it. Well, almost. Her feet squished, catching just part of it.

Rog roared in approval.

Grace wiggled at his sound and moved over a bit. She settled fully on the ground, crunching the warm meat in her mouth. The growling of her stomach slowed. The snap of bones, the warm muscle filled her. Her voracious appetite settling to just normal hunger. Grace bit the last bite, licking her nails clean. She sniffed, turning toward her second deer.

She heard the doctor gagging and from the corner of her eye saw him hurry to the door leading to the facility. Ignoring him, she stretched her neck, she delicately snagged the other deer, pulling it toward her. Her teeth sank into the flesh, enjoying the taste of fresh venison. She sighed, burped and looked at what was left. Glancing around, she found Rog. He sat eating the last of his catch.

Her backpack lay on the ground next to him.

Grace thought about getting dressed and shifted. Suddenly the area was almost too dark to see. The golden gleam of Rog's eyes the only indication of where he sat. She stumbled toward him, hands in front of her. Her fingers touched hard scales, caressed.

Golden eyes locked on hers.

Grace trembled. Her heart fluttering. Suddenly, scales became skin. Warm and hard beneath her fingertips. Smooth beneath her touch. Grace spread her fingers, hands moving up his hard abdomen. Her hands traced his muscled chest, his strong neck, to entwine in his hair, pulling Rog's head down to meet her lips.

She melted against his body. Wind fluttered against her. The other dragons flew away, moving deeper into the forest abutting the meadow. Leaving her and Rog alone in the dark.

His callused hand held her chin in place, deepening their kiss. His tongue entwined with hers.

Grace's legs gave up supporting her. Just his mouth sapped the strength from her body.

Rog followed her down. Hands roaming her body. Lips tracing her curves. Worshipping her.

Her blood caught fire. Grace panted. She stretched, offering every inch of her skin to his lips and tongue. Her mind spun. Heat pooled low in her abdomen.

Rog's fingers gripped her hips, tilting them toward his mouth. Spreading her before him.

Grace's fingers convulsed, grasping at the grass and dirt beside her. She gulped in air at the touch of Rog's tongue tracing her softness. Her chest heaved.

The cool breeze caressed her heated skin.

Grace's head spun.

Rog's lips and tongue teased her, dipping in and out of her body.

She shivered, nipples peaking from the sensations bombarding her. Cream dripped from her body, eagerly licked up by Rog.

One hand slid up her thigh. His fingers traced her lips, rimmed her clit. Slid down and inside her. In and out of her.

Grace moaned, rising to meet his fingers. She panted. A ball of fire filled her. Tension building.

Rog teased her clit with his tongue, making her squirm. He bit down then sucked it in.

Stars burst behind her eyelids, shivers racking her body.

Rog pulled his hand free, forcing a cry from her. He slid up her body, nibbling on his way. At her neck, he sucked.

Grace shivered, mewling.

Rog's hard body covered her. Pressed her into lush grass. He undulated, his cock sliding inside her. Seating himself completely.

Her breath left her. Grace wrapped her legs around him, holding him in. Loving the feel of him deep inside her. She felt each movement, every increment of his cock, gliding in and out of her passage. She tightened on him.

Rog groaned. His hips jerking before he growled. He buried his face in her neck, teeth holding her in place. Rog's gleaming eyes showed his dragon staring back. "Mine."

Excitement slithered through her. Her sight changed, her vision shifting. Her dragon rising. The word slid from her mouth, whispered in the dark. "Yours."

Rog sped up. His pace increasing. His breath rasping with each plunge.

Grace slid in the grass from his force. Arms and legs wrapped around Rog, holding on. Her body heaved, cries bursting from her throat.

His heat, his hard body incited her.

Grace arched picking up Rog's increased rhythm. The staccato thrusting driving her out of her mind. She cried out, nails digging into his back. She tightened, her body drenching with pleasure. Her throat raw, she screamed.

Rog pumped faster, moving erratically. He roared, his cum filling her. Heating her insides and spilling out between them.

"Mine."

Wrapping her arms around his neck, her body satiated, Grace nuzzled his neck. She was so his.

CHAPTER SIXTEEN

Rog rolled over. He reached for Grace but her side of the bed was cold. Grumbling, knowing his morning woody would be unsatisfied, he rumbled his dissatisfaction into the pillow. Inching out of bed, he saw no evidence of Grace.

They'd returned to the same quarters they'd previously used last night. Rog half carried Grace. Each time he picked her up she fought to get down, insisting she could walk. It took twice as long. In the end, she won her way. They stumbled down the corridor until they reached the bedroom.

Where Grace dropped to the bed in a dead sleep.

Rog tucked her under the covers and crawled in beside her. Pulling her to him, he snuggled her. She sighed, tucked her head beneath his, hands folded beneath her head and settled back down. He rumbled, happiness filling him. Arms filled with the other half of his soul, he slept.

But now she was nowhere in sight.

Rog stretched spine cracking. Shuffling into the bathroom he took care of business and stepped into the shower. The warm water slipped down his body, relaxing muscles he didn't realize were so tense. This certainly beat washing in the icy stream. Not as gratifying to his dragon. In his natural form, nothing beat sliding into molten hot lava for burning away dirt and ensuring his scales gleamed.

Turning off the water he emerged. Shaking himself dry, Rog dressed. Time to find Grace.

She wasn't in their living quarters.

He headed down the corridor. Just their presence seemed to imbue life back into the sterile area. He could hear the murmur of voices further down. The sameness of lighting at all hours made it hard to determine what time of day it truly was.

Entering the door, Rog noticed two people sitting down. It appeared as if waking them worked. The doctor was checking out their vitals. Using items from a medical kit sitting next to him. It didn't matter how many centuries passed since he'd been out in the world, it looked like no advancement in the basic equipment had been made. Even the bags containing them were similar. Black carpet bags. Rog snorted.

He grinned. Every head in the room turned toward him. With the exception of Indra. But still no Grace. His smile dropped. "Where's Grace?"

"She went out to practice flying." Indra spoke, his attention still on the woman in the chair.

Rog groaned, realizing Hark was nowhere to be found either. He hurried toward the door leading to the valley. Opening the door, he stepped into the light. Squinting, the sunshine nearly blinding, Rog scanned the horizon.

Heart in his throat, he watched Grace falling. Her wings flapped wildly. Before she was in any real danger, she evened out, roaring in obvious delight.

Hand shading his eyes, Rog watched her land.

Her attempt looked perfect. She didn't roll or stumble on her feet at all. Feet down, she hovered, settling down on all fours. Then she did what he could only call a happy dance.

He chuckled. The gloom of finding her gone from his bed lifted. He'd have her there again. But then he'd have missed her obvious joy.

Grace ran, wings working. She lifted a couple of feet in the air before landing again. Each attempt drove her higher.

Rog thought Hark was with her but didn't see him.

Grace again tried to gain height. Before she started down, Hark swooped in, smoothly grabbing her, assisting her in gaining height and let go. Wings working like crazy, Grace caught an airstream, evening out and gliding into it. She chortled. Flew a loop, flapped to steady herself again and flew around the Valley rim.

Wind smacked Rog, trying to push him over.

Hark landed next to him, shifted, watched Grace fly. "Morning sleepyhead."

"How long has she been learning to fly?"

"Couple of hours." Hark chuckled. "We started with landing. The only way she could really hurt herself was smacking into the ground."

Rog snorted. "Probably a good idea." He watched Grace gliding in a breeze, bringing her back toward them. "She's doing good." He slid a glance at Hark. "Thanks for helping her."

Hark laughed. "Didn't have much of a choice. She kept pestering me until I finally gave in."

Rog frowned. Why didn't she wake him? *Why didn't you wake me to help?*

I wanted to surprise you. Grace swooped overhead. *Aren't I doing well?*

Yes, you are. I saw you land. You're doing very good.

Grace preened above them, wobbled, then straightened out with a giggle. She flew toward the trees, hovered, picking something up and flew back toward him. She dropped a dead cow in front of him.

It hit the ground with a plop.

Breakfast! I caught it myself. Just for you. Did you eat?

Yup, first thing. Grace landed next to it. She ran, looking at him over his shoulder. *I'll figure this part soon enough. I just have to keep trying.*

Rog stripped, and shifted. His dragon delighted in the fact his mate cared enough to feed him. He bit down on her offering, savoring the crush of bones and flesh. He wiggled, enjoying the meal from Grace.

While he ate, Grace continued attempting to leave the ground.

He eyeballed her attempts. She would figure it out. She was doing darn good. Every attempt better than the last. She probably didn't realize she was doing exactly what she needed. Strengthening her wings.

When did you want to head to your home? He hadn't forgot she planned on meeting Lavinia at her home. Better than having her come here and finding out about the facility here and the people waiting to be awakened.

I think the doctor was planning on waking everyone up today. Grace sounded hesitant. Maybe she could guess his thoughts.

Rog growled. He couldn't help it. He didn't want all of them awake. He supposed it wasn't his right to determine. If it was up to him, they would sleep forever. He preferred to claim this area as his weyr. It would keep Grace close to her family if she wanted. The valley lush and able to sustain all of them. With proper husbandry, it would continue to thrive.

But now, with who knows how many people to be awakened, there would be too many humans.

I figured this afternoon. Depending on when she comes, we could always spend the night. Grace purred.

Rog perked up. *I'd love to have you to myself.* He practically drooled at the thought.

Hark nudged him. *I'd like to show you both what I found earlier today. Finish eating. Then you can fuck like bunnies.*

Rog quickly finished off his breakfast, shooting a bit of flame Hark's way. Chuckling when he jumped back. *Dragons not bunnies.* He'd have to start teaching Grace a different path to talk to him. Having Hark listening to every word wasn't ideal. It would come the longer they were mated. That she picked up their common family stream already was impressive. *Thank you for the food, sweetheart.*

Grace nodded, hovering in the air above them.

Let's go. Hark took off, narrowly missing Grace

She took off after him, trying to chase him down. Her eyes bright and smile wide.

Rog laughed and flew after them both. He'd stay behind Grace, making sure she was okay. Plus, the view wasn't bad at all. His dragon followed, perhaps too close, but he couldn't seem not to.

Her scent drew him closer. Rog just wanted to mount her, complete the mating of their dragons in a fantastical aerial mating. Racing across the sky, entwined together. Sealing their bond for life.

Rog flew under Grace, rubbing his head along her belly. He twisted, sliding his belly along hers. His pulse raced. His cock began to extend, seeking her.

We're here. Hark couldn't contain his laughter.

Jackass. Rog flew to the side his groin aching with desire. *Where is here?*

Land and I'll show you. Hark switched his attention. *Grace, can you land here?*

I think so. Grace slowed, spiraling down, slowing with each rotation until she hovered over one spot. Tucking her wings, she landed. Her face glowed, eyes gleaming in joy.

Hark shifted, pulling clothes from a bag he carried.

Rog followed suit. Seeing Grace's garments, he grabbed hers before his own. *Go ahead and shift. I've your clothing.* He watched her concentrate and her human form appeared quickly turning away from the men.

Admiring the view, Rog walked her clothing to her. Sliding a hand to cup a firm buttock and stealing a kiss before he handed them to her.

Her blush rose from her breasts to her cheeks. "Rog!" She grabbed her clothes.

Her jumping around, trying to get into them as quickly as possible did nothing to stop the burn in his groin. Not at all. Her cute little rear wiggling to fill her pants, her bouncing breasts while she concentrated on her bottoms had his breathing labored.

He reached to fill his hands and got a resounding slap on them for trying. Looking at her, giving a little whimper, a pout and widening his eyes, he tried to look forlorn. He hoped she'd let him fondle her for a bit.

Her giggle and eye rolling while she still dressed, covering all the good bits told him he was unsuccessful.

"Might as well put your clothes on." Hark laughed outright at him.

Rog snarled. "Fine." He marched back to his raiment, yanking them on. It was a painful process. His erection did not want to be contained. "Fuck it." Rog headed to the tree line surrounding them. He grabbed his dick, yanking on it. Groaning at his touch, though it wasn't the one he wanted. A few quick pulls and his cum coated the ground in front of him. Turning, he tucked himself in his pants, looking up.

"Oh my god!" Grace's wide eyes and slack jaw faced him. "I can't believe…"

Rog smirked. "It wasn't going down by itself." He grabbed her waist, pulling her toward him. Rubbing his nose against her throat. "I was horny." He grunted, feeling himself harden against her belly. "I'm still horny."

She stirred his blood.

Every time Rog looked at her, his dick rose. Every lick of her lips while she pretended not to be affected by him, every peek from under her lashes made him hard.

"Oh." Even her squeak was cute.

The arousal he could smell from her just made it worse. He convinced himself their sealing of their bond in dragon form would calm him down. Rog knew he was lying to himself. Nothing would stop his desire for her. Each taste made it worse.

But humans weren't like that. And from every indication Grace received very little affection in her life. It had to be overwhelming. But hopefully in a good way.

"Come on. If you two are heading to Grace's place later, let's get this over with. I think you'll like it." Hark stood, hands on his hips, lips pressed together.

Rog thought about how aggravating Ari and Crag were once they met their mates. How he'd done everything he could to tease them. He sobered up, kissing Grace's cheek and releasing her. "Show me."

Hark led the way through the trees, coming to stop at a wide opening in the mountainside. He waved an arm toward it, grinning. "Look what I found." Grabbing a branch, Hark wrapped cloth around it, and lit it with one breath.

Rog grabbed Grace's hand. He preferred to be touching her. He strode forward, noticing the natural cavern. This was no man made mine. The stalactites and stalagmites shown in the limited light, glittering with their natural beauty around the edges of the space.

"It's beautiful." The awe in Grace's voice saw Hark straightening up, pulling back his shoulders.

Rog nodded, agreeing. "Have you explored it?"

"Just a bit. Follow me." Hark took the lead, picking a path through to the next cavern.

A natural water source ran through it. The grotto was warmer than the previous cavern. Rog could see other passages leading from this one. Excitement tickled his belly.

They followed the river deeper into the cave. Smaller caves split from the main branch. It began to warm, the deeper they walked.

Hark stopped, turned to face them. "What do you think?" The elation in his voice obvious.

"I think it's perfect." It was too. The passages would need only a little work to even them out for walking. The smaller caves perfect for families.

"It connects to the facility if you go far enough. It's blocked off, but it's there." Hark snorted. "They used brick."

"What is it perfect for?" Grace looked around.

"A weyr." Rog smiled. His heart racing. Their own weyr. He didn't really want to live in Ari's weyr. Yes, he'd miss Hope and Hark would miss Faith, but it wasn't that far to fly. Rog liked Grace's town much more than Hope's. And the people.

"What's a weyr?" She frowned.

"A dragon home and community." Hark looked around, a smile matching Rog's on his face.

"Wait. We'd live in a cave?" Grace's voice pitched higher than normal.

"Well, we're dragons." Hark cocked his head, looking at her.

"That doesn't mean we won't make it habitable." Rog interjected, back pedaling. "Plus, we need to explore more. Hark did say it connected around to the facility we found." A sense of panic filled him. Grace had to like it. She had to. His dragon was staking out this new territory already.

Grace's eyes narrowed on him. "I'm not sleeping on a rock floor."

Crap.

***

Oh, hell no. Maybe her soddy wasn't up to the standard of the home she'd grown up in, but it had some creature comforts. Like a bed. Sunlight. A breeze. She frowned looking around. An outhouse. Not rock, rock, and more rock.

Maybe she'd been spoiled staying in the living quarters they'd discovered in the mine. But she liked light. Circulation air. Privacy to use the bathroom.

Ugh.

And worse, her dragon totally approved of the dark, moist space they were in. She wanted to cozy up to Rog and rut. The large cavern, the really warm one, she'd marked as a laying ground. Grace wasn't positive what that was, but guessed it had something to do with dragon eggs. Her dragon eagerly agreed. She sighed.

Defeated by her inner self.

She still glared at Rog, not ready to give in, not yet. "I won't move in until it's habitable."

"Change into your dragon and we'll be here tonight." Hark sent her a cheeky grin.

Grace scowled. He was right, but she refused to admit it. The look of panic in Rog's eyes on the other hand made her want to giggle. If he really wanted to move here, she'd do it tomorrow. Today. The cavern behind them looked good enough for a bit of privacy to roll around with her mate. Fire licked her blood.

Forcing her breath to stay even, Grace shook her head.

Hark's snort earned him a sideways glance from both her and Rog.

"I'll make sure we have a bed. A big one." Rog's wagging brows and tempting grin dragged an answering smile from her. "We need to go, though."

Rog slapped a hand on Hark's shoulder. "Great job. This place is perfect." He grabbed her hand, tugging her to him.

Hark beamed, teeth gleaming in the flickering light.

Sliding an arm around Rog's waist, Grace took a deep breath. His musky smell, a mix of fresh air, pine and earth was intoxicating. "Okay, let's go." The cave thrilled the dragon in her. Grace knew she'd lose this battle. But before she gave in, it had to have some sort of creature comforts.

They returned the way they'd come. Soon enough reaching the fresh air.

Grace breathed deeply. Pine, the damp smell of the cavern behind her, earth and water slid through her. It smelled like home. From their location the height of the mountain loomed behind her. Through the trees she could see the valley below. Far below.

"We can stay. You don't have to meet with Lavinia." Rog lay his head on hers, his warm body behind her, arms encircling her waist.

"I can't believe you're related to her." Hark shook his head. "I don't believe it's possible."

"No, I need to talk to her. Find out why she hates me so much." Her breath hitched. The pain of knowing how much she had to hate her to give her up beating down Grace's soul.

"I can't believe I'm saying this, but maybe you should hold judgement until you talk to her." Rog's thoughts were filled with pain.

Her pain, sharing her emotions through their bond. She didn't want that. She needed to remember his joy at finding her. She wanted that. Grace turned, embracing him fully. Her face buried in his chest. "I love you." She pushed her happiness through their bond. *I love you. Nothing means more to you than me. But I need to know.*

Rog nodded. "Then let's do this."

"Follow me." Hark led the way up. His path wound a bit, but always headed up. A short time later, a flat ledge gave ample room.

The men stripped and shifted. They turned and looked at her.

With a snort, Grace faced away from them, stripped, shoved her clothes in Hark's bag and shifted. *Now what?*

Now we fly! Hark ran forward leaping off the ledge.

Rog joined him. His wingspan enormous. The backdraft enough to knock her off her feet if she'd been on two rather than four.

Grace watched in awe. Their scales gleamed in the sunlight. She sighed, wonder filling her at the sight. To imagine that dragons were a thing. So amazing to watch.

Laughter filled her mind. *But so much more amazing to join us, flying over the world. Seeing the world in a way you never imagined. Come, join us.* Rog's deep voice in her mind threatened to turn her knees to water.

It was a good thing she was stronger than that. Grace snorted. Ran forward and taking a leap of faith, and a deep breath, jumped off the cliff. Pumping her wings, she fell, then slowly rose. She gave a whoop only it came out as a roar. Happy, no disguising that, but a roar of triumph all the same.

She flew. She flew! No one carrying her into the air and letting her go. She did it. All by herself. Grace twisted, spiraling in the sky. An air current caught her, aiding in keeping her aloft.

Hark and Rog flew alongside her. Their body language declaring their pride and protectiveness.

Grace looked around her. Below, far below, the cattle appeared to be ants. Even the mountain looked small in comparison to their altitude. If there were people down there, she couldn't see them. The trees looked like toothpicks. The valley below larger than she'd assumed. She circled. Their mountain. She grinned. Yes, their mountain.

The valley became a forest, then another meadow. Flying, heading toward another mountain, Grace realized this valley was the one attached to the facility.

Circling, she gazed back the way they'd come. Looking at the mountains. She could see their mountain. Their entrance was on the other side of the mountain range. The enormous valley separated from the one attached to the facility. The mountains appeared to be one range or perhaps two that abutted. Hark's claim the two cave systems met made sense.

Looking closer, Grace could see the difference in the areas. The valley near the facility they'd found looked tame. If not manmade, then definitely engineered for efficiency. The river, while wild, could have been redirected. The way it flowed, separating the meadow, kept the animals from mingling over much. It could only have been done by man.

Admittedly, since human hands hadn't been around in centuries, it had gone wild. What might have once been fields for planting would have to be tamed. Looking back, Grace filled with elation. Their valley was wild. Game filled. Even room to till. If say, her family was interested. If not, they were easily close enough to fly back to visit.

Like what you see? Rog intruded in her silence.

It's like nothing I ever expected. Grace flew close enough to rub her head against his. *It's obvious from here that this place was planned. The river's not natural. At least not its path.*

Hark nodded. *I have to agree. It's obvious this was a government facility.*

They passed over the last of the valley were the chickens squawked, wandering around and scratching in the dirt.

It won't take long to get to my soddy.

They circled the mountain top. It seemed strange to think people were hidden below in the mountain. Bodies, sleeping away the centuries. Grace shivered. Someone walked over her grave. At least, that's what her mother called it. Her throat tightened. Grandmother.

Despite the fresh air filling her lungs, they hurt. Like she couldn't breathe. An ache burned at the back of her eyes. Hell, her nostrils stung. And it wasn't from the wind streaming past her face.

Sorrow filled her. Grace thought her mom was just tired from being so old when she bore her. Not that she was forced to watch someone else's baby while being unable to mourn her own. Who would ever think such a thing?

Grace cried out, letting out her sorrow, her rage, her helplessness. Her eyes widened. Flames she hadn't meant to ignite burned from her jaws. She snapped her jaws shut, backpedaling. Staring where the flames were. She ducked her head, glancing up at Rog from under her lashes. "Oops."

Rog's snort and Hark's laughter tugged a grin to her lips.

"So, that's how you make fire." Rog smirked; his teasing eased the ache in her heart.

CHAPTER SEVENTEEN

Grace stared at him, eyes not blinking, then mischief filled her gaze, laughter spilling out.

Rog watched the emotions zip across his mate's face. His heart ached, knowing he couldn't just fix everything for her. He could be there for her. Tease her out of her tantrums and doldrums.

She was strong. The news from her grandmother shocking her to her soul. He'd seen every inch of her hurt and confusion on her expressive face. She would be okay. He would make sure of it. Soon enough their bond would strengthen. He would feel every bit of her emotions, then. He wished they were close enough already for him to share her burden.

Thinking of the coming meeting must have sunk in. The rage on her face, her hurt expression twisted his gut, until she'd surprised herself. Her owl eyed expression feeding his amusement when she'd ignited her flames.

"Want to try it again?" Rog circled her, tilting his head, looking at her.

"No." Grace scrunched her nose. "How did I do that, anyway?"

"Anger, probably. Wanting to protect yourself. Self-preservation will trigger our fire. But, it's controllable." Rog flew next to her, brushing a wingtip down her jaw line.

"Yes, or Indra would have burnt the facility down already." Hark's dry comment pulled a smile to Grace's face.

"What do you mean? What's up with Indra?" Rog looked at Hark.

"The doctor is a bit bossy. He doesn't like Indra hanging around." Hark snickered. "I think he's trying to get Indra away from his daughter."

Rog snorted. "He'll have no luck there." Rog flew around Grace. "Want to try before we get to your house? Just shoot a little flame at Hark over there. He's a big target."

"Hey." Hark chuckled. "None of that."

"Maybe later." Grace started moving. "I have a meeting to go to."

Rog nodded. They passed the mine entrance. Flew past the steep path leading up. Soon enough the trees were gathering around the river below.

Grace slowed, arcing over the meadow.

Rog looked closer. Below the signs of habitation were obvious if you looked for them. Part of the meadow appeared to be a garden in the middle of nowhere. It was next to the soddy, off to the side of what Rog assumed was the door.

Dark spots showed some types of construction, perhaps a smoke house or animal pens.

The more he looked, the more he saw. In the middle of the garden sat a dark rectangle. Near it, Rog could see the figure of a man.

Nearby, the river he and Hark had played in flowed by close enough to easily supply water to Grace's home. *I wonder why Walter is here.* Grace moved up, leaving plenty of distance between him and her.

Walter?

Lavinia's brother. That's him below. I wonder what he's up to?

Rog nodded, watching him. Trying to figure out what he was doing. *He's digging.* The distance was too great to see what exactly he was digging.

Or burying.

Rog flew in closer, close enough to see. Digging, he was digging.

Why on earth would he be digging here? Grace frowned.

It looks like a grave. Hark slowly spoke. *It's not the only one either.* He waved a leg, pointing with his talons.

Rog looked. Hark was right. The dark spot he'd seen was a second hole, body sized, a couple of feet from the one he currently was digging. *That makes no sense whatsoever. Why would he be digging two graves?*

I think we should land and surprise him. Grace slowed, starting her landing procedure. *Ask him.*

No, wait. Hark, grab him. Rog sniffed. The closer they got, the more the scent of blood assaulted his nostrils. *Don't let him go. I don't like this.*

Rog knew something wasn't right. The blood was fresh.

Hark dove out of the air, snatching Walter from the ground.

Rog chuckled at the feminine shriek he emitted. Rog landed, running into what must surely be Grace's home. He stopped, staring at the sight in front of him.

Grace followed right behind him. Shifting on the run.

He was too late to stop her from seeing.

Grace screamed, diving to the body lying on the floor in a pool of blood. "Lavinia." Her hands slipped in the blood.

Bring your first aid kit, hurry. Rog moved to Grace's side. It didn't look good.

What should I do with this person? Hark grunted.

Drop him in one of the holes he dug. Bury him. Just leave his head out. If you can. It would serve him right if he suffocated in the grave he dug. Rog ground his teeth.

"Grace, let me look." Rog moved her over a bit. "Look, she's breathing. Let us save her."

"Can you?" Grace's breath rushed out of her.

"Give me room and let me see." Rog nudged her further away.

He checked Lavinia's body. Lips pressed together, he rumbled. Brushing her clothing away, he found stab wounds in her shoulders, her arms and legs. A head wound contributing the most to the blood pool.

Beneath those, bruising. Some black and new. Many showing yellowing, declaring they'd been there a while. Scars marred her skin. Running his hands down her legs and arms, Rog detected the poorly healed bones. His stomach clenched.

Grace gasped at the sight of the abuse. "Oh my God."

"Ignore all that. Let's save her. If she doesn't stop bleeding, she might not make it." Rog looked at Grace. "Do you have something we could bandage her with? And hot water to clean her wounds."

Hark slid in the door. "I've got my bag." He dropped it on the floor. "She going to make it?"

"I think so. We need to sew her up." Rog shook his head. "Why would he do this?"

"You think it was Walter." Grace stood, gripping a jug. Her knuckles white around the handle.

"Yes. He had blood on him. Go get some water. We need to clean her wounds to prevent infection." Rog slid over, giving room to Hark. Of the two of them, he was better at doctoring.

"Hurry woman." Hark waved at the door. "No time to waste."

"I'll get the water. Get something for bandages." Rog grabbed the jug, shooing Grace. He ran to the river, filling the jug with icy water. Carrying it back to the house he saw Grace shoving wood in a stove. Beside her on a chair, a large white cloth was piled.

Rog moved Grace, pulling her back. He leaned over and breathed on the logs, instantly setting them crackling. He poured the water into a pan on the stove, moving it over the flames.

"I didn't think of doing that." Grace whispered.

Rog pulled her into her arms. "She's going to be okay, sweetheart." He hugged her. For her sake Rog hoped he was speaking true. "Now, let's get these bandages ready for Hark."

Grace nodded, pulling from his arms. She grabbed the cloth and started tearing it in strips.

Relieved she was moving, Rog turned to the water and breathed fire into it. It began to boil.

"Perfect. Bring it here." Hark had moved Lavinia, stripping her outer clothing from her and laying her on Grace's bed. "And some of those bandages. Now." He snapped his fingers.

Grace startled. Jumped a bit and brought the torn-up material to him.

Rog shifted his hands, protecting them with scales and carried the water over. No time to find something to protect his human hands.

Hark dipped some of the scraps in the water and began to wash Lavinia's wounds. "Get the needle and thread ready. She needs to be sewed up. Rog, get me some aloe. The tin is marked."

Grace grabbed her sewing kit, pulling out both.

Rog opened Hark's bag, rummaging in it. Finding what he wanted, Rog brought it over along with the medicine to help prevent infection. At least, it worked on dragons.

Hark tossed the rags to the floor, grabbing the threaded needle from Grace. He dipped it in the boiling water. Rog began to rub the aloe over the wounds he could see. Lifting her arms to get both sides of the stab wounds.

Hark began to sew them up.

Lavinia stirred, crying out. Thrashing against the pain.

Rog held her down. "It's okay. We just need to stop the bleeding."

Her cries tore his heart up. Rog looked up.

Grace sat, holding down Lavinia's legs, tears dripping silently down her cheeks.

"I love you." How could he not say it? Grace's tears had him wanting to beat his chest and tear apart anything that made her cry.

Her shaky smile, despite her tears, lifted his spirit. They'd get through this. Patch up Lavinia. Figure out what happened.

Rog decided that Walter was one long drop away from justice. The blood on his clothes declared him guilty of this heinous crime. The double graves more evidence of the harm he planned. He didn't think Grace had thought it through. Rog was in no doubt, the second grave had been planned for Grace.

Rage tore through him. His teeth pressed against his gums, growing. His nails switching to talons in an instance. Rog took a deep breath, forcing it back in. His hands shook. Suppressing any emotion was hard. Normally, laughing and pranking his siblings was as deep as he got.

The tumultuous emotions raging through him right now were unfamiliar. His love for Grace was easy. She filled his heart and soul with light. The dark feelings swirling in him now, calling for revenge, simmered. Boiled. Demanded justice.

Walter would pay.

"Once she's sewed up, can we take her to see the doctor?" Grace cleared her throat.

"In town?" Rog figured he could drop Walter on the way.

"No, to the facility. Steven should be able to help."

"Time is all she will need. I think." Hark added. "But we could care for her there easier. And it wouldn't hurt to see if the doc can make sure she doesn't have internal injuries." He threaded the needle again, blowing on the water to reheat it. Once it boiled, he dipped the needle and thread in again. Then started stitching another laceration. Even with Hark's healing abilities, there were no guarantees.

Rog supposed having lifesaving equipment and knowledge would be a good thing. The facility had more mysteries yet to be explored and he bet there was a medical facility there somewhere, more than just the cryonics laboratory.

Rog's stomach turned. Seeing the injuries from her own brother, he wondered if the bruises were from him too. Looking at Grace and back to Lavinia he thought he had an idea of why she'd given up her own baby to someone else to raise.

***

Grace watched Hark repair Lavinia's skin. Each stitch neat. She doubted they'd even leave a scar. Her eyes wandered. Not that it would matter. She swallowed. Lavinia had plenty already. And the bruises. Grace couldn't even begin to imagine.

Being raised by her grandparents didn't seem so bad.

"Grace." Lavinia's scream brought her head up. She was thrashing, delirious. "No, not Grace."

Rog pressed her harder to the bed, limiting her movements.

Lavinia moaned, tears rolling down her cheeks. "Stop. Stop."

Hark sat back. "Roll her over. I need to mend any wounds on her back."

Rog and Hark slowly moved Lavinia to her stomach.

Her cries tore at Grace's heart.

Luckily, if you wanted to call it that, she only had one wound that still needed stitching. It looked like the knife had gone clean through her. Grace knew stitching her obvious wounds would only help so much. Time would tell if her injuries were too severe for Lavinia's survival. Maybe the doctor could tell. Perhaps not all of the equipment in the facility they found should be hoarded.

Grace stifled a sob, holding down Lavinia, her mother's legs.

Her mother.

Looking at her, seeing the bruises, the scars decorating her body, Grace couldn't hold the hate in her heart anymore. There had to be an explanation why she'd given her up. Why her grandmother was willing to hide the death of her own child and raise another in their place. Grace was pretty sure the evidence of why was laid bare in front of her.

"Done." Hark stood up, stretching his back. "Let's put her back on her stomach. Most of the wounds are there and they'll heal faster that way." He and Rog carefully rolled her over. "I'm going to check on Walter."

"We can make a litter and carry her back."
Rog eased off the bed, careful not to jostle Lavinia.
He traced a finger over Grace's cheek. "Are you all right?"

She nodded. "I think so."

"Good." Rog smiled into Grace's eyes. "We'll go deal with Walter and make a litter to carry Lavinia."

Grace nodded. Again. Shaking herself she fought to get out of her head. Things had to happen. Curling up crying wouldn't help. Didn't matter if it was for her mother or herself. "Yes." Grace grabbed his arm. "I want to take Walter to the sheriff. He needs to pay."

Rog's lips tightened. "Are you sure? I could just as easily drop him." His eyes glanced skyward. "From there. Really, really high up there."

Her lips twitched. Grace let the smile out. "As much as I'd like to have that happen, I'd like the whole town to know what he did. And watch him pay." She frowned. "Where is he?"

"Still here." The satisfaction in Hark's voice had Grace hurrying outside. Thankfully the holes he dug were not directly in front of her door.

She laughed. Walter's pale face and wide eyes were the only part of his body Grace could see

Walter's face gained color at the sound of her laugh. He turned his head, hate filling his eyes. He glared at her.

Grace stepped back at the look in his eyes.

"I hope she's dead." Spittle flew from his mouth. Much like the hate spewing from his mouth. The rest of him buried in the dirt right where he'd been digging.

"Then you'll die for it." Grace kicked dirt in his face. Satisfaction filled her at his curses.

Rog chuckled. "Really high, sweetheart. Just let me know if you change your mind."

Grace shook her head. She went back in to check on her mother. She wondered if she said it enough it would seem real.

"Grace." The whisper drew her attention to Lavinia.

"Lavinia." Grace sat on the floor next to the bed. Her head even with her mother's so she didn't have to move.

"Get away. Walter. Hurt you." Lavinia could barely speak.

The worry in her eyes hurt Grace's heart. She smoothed a hand over Lavinia's hair. "He can't. The men have him in hand."

"Dangerous."

"No more. We're taking him to the sheriff." Grace looked into her eyes. "He won't get away with this. And when you're better, we need to talk."

Lavinia nodded, just barely. Her eyes traced Grace's face. "You look so much like your father." She sighed and her eyes closed.

Grace's pulse leaped. But the rise and fall of her chest assured Grace she lived.

"We're done." Rog stuck his head in the door. "Are you doing okay sweetheart?"

"Yes. Better than expected." She stood up. Walked to the door and kissed Rog. His lips were firm under hers. Just the simple touch ignited a fire between her thighs. "I need to make sure the stove will die out safely."

Grace headed over to it. She could feel Rog's eyes on her. She swayed just a bit more than normal on her way across the room. The man lit her body on fire. She grabbed a poker and pushed the logs inside the stove apart to break the fire. Making sure nothing nearby could ignite, she closed it down. It would smolder for a while but extinguish on its own.

Rog and Hark entered her house carrying a litter for Lavinia.

It was larger than Grace thought it needed to be. When she saw them lift the mattress rather than her mother, she realized why.

They placed the mattress carefully on the litter.

Lavinia didn't even stir.

"How are we going to get Walter to town?" Grace chewed on her lip.

"The question is how are we going to get Lavinia and Walter to town. She'll have to be seen for the sheriff to believe us." Hark sat in the lone chair by the table.

"We could go at dark. There is room to land near the sheriff's office." Rog frowned. "I don't want to be seen. Not my dragon at least."

"That sounds like the best idea. Grace you can lead the way. I can carry the litter. Rog you can carry Walter." Hark leaned back, rocking on the rear legs of the chair. "Sound good?"

"Will you be able to land?" Grace wondered if he'd land on top of Lavinia. She'd had enough problems without being flattened by a dragon.

"Don't doubt me, little sister. She'll be perfectly safe with me." His smirk actually relieved her. If he was joking, there was nothing to worry about.

"In the meantime, how about some food?" Rog checked on Lavinia.

She slept soundly.

"Hark, can you stay here? Just in case there is a problem with Walter. I'm taking Grace hunting. I don't want Lavinia left alone with him."

Grace started to protest, but the determination in Rog's eyes stifled it. She needed practice hunting anyway.

"We can head into the trees. I don't want Walter seeing our dragons." Rog strode off toward the herd and their feeding grounds.

"Uh, grabbed him as a dragon, bro!" Hark hollered after him.

Grace glanced back at Walter and hurried after Rog. Walter was the last person she'd trust, but it was too late, he'd already seen Hark. Not to mention, neither Rog nor Hark had protested flying so close to the town to get justice. Maybe it wouldn't matter.

Once surrounded, they shifted, bringing out their dragons. Grace ran across the field, climbing up a rock and launching herself off it. To her delight, she stayed aloft. Her wings seemed stronger. Maybe that was the difference.

She flew, not toward the herd, but toward the woods. Grace knew the deer tended to gather there. Slipping through the trees, Grace finally caught the scent of deer. She followed the scent to the small meadow they used. A couple of deer were grazing close to her. Easing up on them, she snatched one in each claw, using her talons to slay them instantly.

Grace wasn't even sure the herd realized. Rising, she darted back into the trees. Both her kills were older deer. Even if they'd seen her, she'd have caught them. Grace's stealth just kept the herd from running.

She flew back toward her house, keeping of out Walter's line of sight. She dropped both deer on the ground.

Hark, I've deer behind the house for you. Grace turned following her exact path back. She might be able to get a deer for herself too. The herd should still be there.

Thank you. You beat Rog? The amusement in his voice startled a chuckle from her.

Evidently. Now to grab one for myself.

Happy hunting. Hark's mirth had her bouncing back toward the herd.

Flying through the trees, definitely an advantage of her smaller size, Grace eyed the herd. A few hundred yards, a lone deer stood grazing. Closer than the rest to the trees, Grace maneuvered her way around. Hovering for a moment, she quickly zipped out and pounced on the animal. Her talons snapped its neck and she flew back into the trees.

Grace landed gently with her catch. Settling in the tall grass, she quickly devoured her prey. She didn't have a huge appetite today. The one alone filled her.

Grace stretched. She hadn't seen Rog since he'd taken off. She found it hard to believe she'd found game before he had. Standing, Grace looked around. Still no Rog.

Trotting into the meadow, Grace increased her speed. Beating her wings, she ran faster. Flapping faster. Finally, she rose. Slowly, but still. She continued until she flew near the treetops. Then each beat of her wings kept her aloft.

Glee filled her. Flying. Absolutely something she'd never thought of doing but couldn't imagine not doing anymore.

A shadow crossed her. Grace flipped, flying upside down, ogling the sexy dragon above her.

He skimmed the trees, making straight toward her. His eyes intent on her.

Grace flipped, pushing herself harder. Instinctively running. If he wanted her, he had to catch her.

They circled the field. Each feint from him was then countered. Up and down over the treetops and skimming the grass.

Grace turned, seeking the trees when he caught her. She tried bucking him off.

His grip tightened. His tail wrapped around hers, capturing her. His neck twined with hers. His rumbling sending a shiver from her head to her tail.

Grace softened, bucking one last time. After all he caught her fair and square. She was now his to do with as he pleased.

CHAPTER EIGHTEEN

Hark set Lavinia gently down on the ground. He hovered and moved to her side. Shifting, he quickly dressed.

Rog dropped Walter. He'd hit him over the head with a shovel to knock him out. A light tap, but it sure made him feel better. Rog shifted and got dressed as Walter stirred. Grabbing the rope he'd brought from Grace's home, Rog hog tied him.

Grace landed and tossed on clothing she'd taken from her home. "If you two want to wait here, I'll get the sheriff."

Before he could stop her, Grace was down to the street. She crossed the roadway from the cemetery where they landed to the sheriffs.

She knocked on the door.

A large man opened it. He waved Grace in, but she shook her head.

She talked, waving her hands around. She pointed toward the cemetery.

The man nodded and followed Grace over.

"See. Here's Walter. There is still blood on his clothes." Grace pointed.

"I see lots of dirt." The man got close to Walter, tugging on his shirt. Sniffed it. "Yup, that's blood."

"Look at Lavinia. He stabbed her multiple times." Grace stifled a sob. "He left her lying in a pool of blood and he was outside digging a grave. A second grave."

"Why would either of them be out at your place?" The sheriff stood, walked over to Lavinia. Pulling the sheet from over her, he squatted down. Running a finger over the stitches. His mouth tightened, twitched down at the corners.

"She came to warn me." Grace's brows seemed glued together, the worry in her face evident.

To Rog, since they'd completed their mating in the meadow, Grace's feelings were obvious. Worry, frustration and anger beat at her, easily felt through their bond.

"Why would she do that?" He stood, covering Lavinia back up.

Grace sighed. "Turns out, Lavinia is my mother." She looked at Lavinia, gnawing on her lip. "Guess she didn't hate me after all."

Rog bit his lip to keep his laugh in. The sheriff's eyes nearly bugged out of his head.

"Why don't we take this to my office." He picked up Walter by the ropes. Ignoring the groans and swearing coming from him, dragged him out of the cemetery and across the road.

Rog and Hark took the litter and carried it between them, careful not to jostle their load. Grace ran up the steps, holding the door wide. Rog looked for a place to set Lavinia down, but Grace was already holding open another door. Rog could see a large table and a couch, perfect to balance their load.

Setting the head on the couch cushions and the feet on the table it left Lavinia at a height where she could place her feet on the ground and sit. If she could sit up. Rog doubted she'd have the strength for a while.

The sheriff tossed Walter in a cage in back, locking the door.

He came back, sitting in a chair near Lavinia.

"So, explain what happened." He stared at Grace.

Grace sat on the edge of another couch.

Rog joined her.

Hark sat on the last chair.

Grace cleared her throat. "Yesterday, my mom told me Lavinia was my real mother. Turns out Lois is my grandmother. Lavinia is my mom and…"

"Peter is your dad." He pursed his lips and stared off. "Makes sense."

"Then I decided I wanted an explanation. So, Paul went over to Lavinia's but she wouldn't come back with him. She told him she'd come see me today at my soddy." Grace stared at the floor. "I didn't know when she'd get there, but knowing how long it took from town, I figured she'd be there in the afternoon." Her lip quivered.

"We got there and found Walter digging a hole. A second hole. Body sized." Rog snorted. "We didn't know what he was doing there."

"I snuck up and smacked him in the head with a shovel and tied him up." Hark added. "I wasn't gentle. That's probably part of where the dirt came from. We could see the blood on him easily in the daylight."

It was believable and they'd decided to keep their dragons out of the story. Walter would just look insane talking of dragons.

"I went into Grace's home and she followed me before I could stop her." Rog slid his arm around Grace, pulling her under his shoulder.

"Lavinia lay in a puddle of blood. Stab wounds all over her." Grace sobbed, turning her face into my chest. "She told me to run, there was danger. Yet, there she was, dying on the floor in front of me."

"I checked her out, Grace tore up bandages, and Rog heated up water. Once she was clean and salve on her wounds, we headed here." Hark crossed his legs, leaning back in the chair.

A sob came from Lavinia. "He murdered Peter. Buried him in the forest. I couldn't take the chance of him finding out my baby lived. He beat me, trying to make me lose my baby. I ran away, hid out with Peter's parents. No one knew where I was. Then, Lois went into labor. I did too." She coughed.

The sheriff stood and poured a glass of water. He held it to Lavinia's mouth, letting her sip.

She licked her lips. "When Lois's baby died, we said it was mine. She knew about Walter. Peter told her. Told her how cruel Walter had always been. There was something wrong with him but my parents ignored it. Ignored the bruises and broken bones when he beat on me. Swearing it was all my fault. I begged her to raise Grace. The thought of Walter hurting her, possibly killing her, horrified me. Lois suggested we say her son was mine since he was born dead."

Grace moved toward Lavinia, grabbing her hand.

Lavinia clutched Grace's hand. "I couldn't bear to ever have Walter suspect. So, I was as mean as I could be to you." Her voice dropped. "It tore me up. But I swear he would have taken your life." She groaned. "He heard Paul when he came over. Swore to kill us both. I ran, went to your soddy, but you never came home. But I knew you'd come to talk to me, so I waited."

Grace bit her lip. Tears slipping down her face. She looked at me, heartbreak in her eyes. Regret obvious for not being there in time to stop Walter. "I'm sorry."

"S'okay." Lavinia looked at the sheriff. "Walter stabbed me. Furious I was there. Furious I lied all those years." Lavinia hiccupped.

The sheriff's face got grimmer with each word from Lavinia's mouth. "I won't let Walter out." He turned to Rog. "I'll need to see Grace's home."

Rog nodded. "The blood is still there. And the holes in the yard."

"Grace, I'll need to talk to your mother, er, grandmother to substantiate the story."

Grace wiped her eyes. "Yes. If she told all of us, she should be willing to talk to you. Papa will too. He knew about it. He was mad she told me."

"Okay. I can help you take Lavinia home." The sheriff stood.

"No. I don't want her there. We have a friend that's a doctor. We were going to take her to him to watch over." Grace looked down the hall where Walter was yelling. "If he did this to her at home, she shouldn't ever go back there. How can her family have let it happen?"

"If I need to talk to her again, how can I reach you?" The sheriff asked.

"We're up near the old mine, but you can tell Paul. We can get back here the same day if necessary." Rog shook the sheriff's hand.

"It might be later at night, depending on when he reaches us." Grace said. "I don't think I can ever live in my house again." She shuddered.

Rog hugged Grace to him. He wished he could take away everything she learned. The weight of her sorrow making his heart ache.

I'll always be here for you.

Grace hugged him tighter. *I love you.*
I love you too.

***

They carried Lavinia out, the sheriff watching them. No one else was around. Dark blanketed the area. They stopped when the door shut, closing off the light from inside.

Lavinia squealed when she saw Hark and Rog strip. She gasped and fainted when they shifted into dragons. She didn't notice Grace strip and shift. It was probably better that way.

Hark lifted off. He moved above the litter, his wing muscles bulging lowering to pick it up. He then slowly gained altitude before flying off toward the mines.

Grace gawked at the sheer power in his form.

"Hey, you should be looking at me like that, not my brother." Rog nuzzled her face. "You're mine."

Grace nuzzled him back. "I had no idea how much restraint and power a dragon had."

"Forget restraint from me." Rog laughed. "I have none where you're concerned."

Her tummy twisted. Her loins heated.

Rog took a deep breath, his eyes gleaming.

Her cheeks heated too. Grace ducked her head, launching into the air. Her eyes widened. "I did it." She did a victory dance. Admittedly it was in the air, so probably looked a bit spastic, but whatever.

Rog followed her up, encouraging her to gain more height.

She sped up because his encouragement consisted of nips to her tail and his tongue tickling her. Grace stifled her giggle and flew faster.

They flew over town, saving a little time. It was too dark to see them with their black scales. Finally, they reached the mine entrance. Just a little further. They flew over the mountain, landing near the back entrance to the facility. Outside were Zeru and Indra. Indra stared at the door with a brooding expression on his face.

Hark set Lavinia down. Her injuries were no longer life threatening since they'd stopped the bleeding. But she had lots of healing to do before she returned to normal.

Rog and Hark flew off.

Grace landed and shifted, dressing quickly. She was beginning to understand how the men could be so casual about being nude. Shifting and hiding while getting dressed was beginning to be a pain in the ass. She headed to Lavinia. Grace was glad she still slept.

Zeru and Indra looked at Lavinia, turning to Grace.

"What is this?" Zeru looked at Lavinia.

Grace saw his eyes roam over the bandages and bruises showing. She noticed his nostrils flare and eyes narrow.

"Who did this?" Zeru glared, like Grace had hurt her.

"Her brother. We took him to the sheriff. We brought my mother here to see if the doctor could keep an eye on her. Make sure she doesn't get any infections. I thought she had a better chance here than with the doctor in town." Grace knew the doctor in town preferred home remedies and was more of an herbalist. The only training doctors had now was on hand training and what they read in old books. Much of the equipment and medicines weren't available.

But Grace bet they were here. So, here is where she wanted to get to know her mother.

We're getting food. Did Zeru and Indra need any? Rog's voice filled her head.

Grace wondered why Rog and Hark flew off but was too intent on her mother to question it. His question explained it without her having to ask.

"Did you two need any dinner? Rog and Hark are hunting." Grace inquired.

"I'll join them." Indra stripped, shifted and flew off.

You might as well bring me and Zeru some. I'm hungry and Indra is joining you.

"What's wrong with him?" Grace grabbed the sheet and blanket over Lavinia, straightening them from the wind from Indra's wings.

Zeru laughed. "Mating isn't going so well."

Grace rolled her eyes. She could see that. If Rog hadn't rescued her, she might not be too keen on believing in dragons.

A thud sounded next to her. Grace jumped, a hand flying to her heart.

Rog hovered, a mischievous grin on his face and a cow carcass at her side. *Eat, love.*

Grace smiled. A second body crashing down next to her didn't get the same reaction.

For Zeru. His laughter sounded in her mind.

"Looks like dinner is here." She waved her hands toward the carcasses. Grace noticed the fire was burning. She hadn't paid attention earlier. She pulled the cow over near the fire, skinning and spitting it. She didn't want to strip and shift again and again tonight. Plus, if Lavinia woke, there would be food for her. Grace tossed the skin over a tree branch and rinsed off in the stream.

Zeru was crunching behind her. His sky-blue dragon quickly devouring the meat. A second landed next to him.

Indra landed, scarfing down his catch.

Hark and Rog landed with their prey dropping just before them.

Rog tossed another carcass to Grace.

Glancing from the fire to the meat laying there, Grace tossed her hands in the air and stripped. Her hunger getting the best of her. She shifted. The smell drawing her closer. Eyeing up the male dragons, she hooked a talon in the beast, pulling it to her. Settling down, Grace savored the flavor. She batted her eyes at Rog.

Lavinia slept, not moving.

The dragons feasted on their game, the aroma of roasting meat filling the air. The door opened from the facility. A gasp brought all eyes to it.

Standing framed in the door was the doctor's daughter, her eyes wide and mouth agape. Her hands clutched her chest. "You weren't lying." Then she crumpled, eyes rolling to the back of her head.

Indra shifted running and catching her before she hit the ground. He looked around helplessly. "What am I supposed to do now?"

Grace snorted in amusement. "I'd lay her down." When Indra started to lay her right there in the dirt, she shook her head. "In a bed. Not here."

Indra scooped her up and went inside.

Zeru was the first to laugh.

The rest of them joined in.

The doctor looked out, then seeing Lavinia laying there turned his head, yelling for Tony. Evidently that was his son. They came out, and lifted the litter, taking her inside.

Grace gulped down the last of her meat, shifted, quickly dressed and followed them. "That's my mother. She's been stabbed."

Setting Lavinia down on the floor in the corner of the cryonic room, the doctor examined her. "She's been treated."

"Yes, but I want to make sure she doesn't get an infection. I thought there would be medicines here that are no longer available. Plus, we don't know if she has internal injuries." Grace sighed. "I just found her. I don't want to lose her."

Steven nodded. He pulled up the sheet, covering her back up. "That shouldn't be a problem." He turned to Grace. "This is my son, Tony. He's an electrical engineer."

"Nice to meet you." Grace shook his hand. What the heck was an electrical engineer?

Tony laughed, obviously reading the confusion on her face. "I work with lighting and systems that run on electric." He waved his arm around the room. "I helped set up the light systems and ways for this place to keep running while we were incapacitated."

An arm slid around her waist.

Grace melted into Rog's side, wrapping her arm around his. Tingles ran through her body. "Can you watch over my mother while she heals?"

Steven nodded. "She'll be fine here while I continue to wake up everyone."

Rog cleared his throat. "We were thrilled to find this place, but it's obvious those that wake up will have claim to it. But we like it here."

"You can move into one of the unclaimed quarters. Not everyone made it." Steven looked at the pods still beeping. "I don't know what went wrong."

"No, we prefer our own quarters. We like our space. But Grace likes some of your amenities." Rog sighed, squeezing Grace's waist. "Would you be able to set up the lighting system and a few others in our weyr?"

Tony shrugged. "It shouldn't be a problem. It's a combination of solar and wind power. Easy really. We should have enough supplies. I'd be happy to." He grinned. "After all, if it wasn't for you, we would still be sleeping."

"Thank you." Grace squeaked.

Rog swept her up in his arms. "Then if you can keep a watch on Lavinia, I think it's time we turned in."

"I'll check her out, make sure there is nothing more wrong with her. Tamara can help me. She's a medical doctor."

"Thank you. I'll be back to see how she is. There's meat roasting on the fire." Grace tossed over Rog's shoulder. "Help yourself."

Rog's arms wrapped around her body, cuddling her to him. He strode rapidly down the corridor.

Heat filled her. Any touch from Rog lit her fuse. She tossed her arms around his neck, burying her face in his neck.

His arms tightened around her, then one hand turned a knob. "I'll make our weyr everything you want." His voice hoarse.

Grace looked up at him, drowning in his eyes. "You're everything I want."

His lips descended, covering hers.

Heat exploded, coursing through her body.

"Mine." He rumbled against her lips.

Yes. His. Forever.

Epilogue

Satisfaction shot through Grace. She watched Walter's body swing. It had taken time to see justice win. But she did it. The body swaying in the breeze attested to that fact.

Grace let the hatred for all Walter had stolen from her drift away. She had Rog. His family. Her family. Looked down at her belly. Their family.

Rog held her to him, his arm around her waist. His steadfast support deepening her love for him every day. Just his arm around her made her want to climb him.

Grace chuckled. That would be quite a sight.

Grace turned from Walter's body to the loving woman on her arm. She realized Walter hadn't stolen anything. Delayed it a bit, but no matter what he did Lavinia's love for Grace had always been there, from the day of her birth.

Lavinia seemed a changed woman. She glowed now acting like the mother Grace always wished she had. Lavinia had struck up a flirtation with Doctor Steven that made her blossom. She agreed once their home was ready, she'd move in with Grace and Rog.

Seeing the intensity between her mother and the doctor, Grace somehow doubted it.

"It's over." The relief she felt made her sag a bit, hugging Rog's arm.

Lavinia leaned in and hugged her. "You're right." Releasing Grace's arm, she looked at them both. She kissed Grace on her cheek and hugged Rog. Then Lavinia turned, walking toward her parents. She'd moved back to town, wanting to take care of her parents.

Grace swallowed her resentment. They let Walter become the man he was. Despite their fragility, she refused to talk to them. But Lavinia's promise to move closer soothed Grace.

"Mom." Grace still couldn't believe the joy she felt saying that.

Lavinia stopped, looking at Grace over her shoulder.

"I need to tell her." Grace told Rog. She ran, grabbing Lavinia's arm. Grace whispered in her ear.

The joy blooming across Lavinia's face said it all. She threw her arms around Grace, hugging her and crying. She pulled back, kissed Grace's forehead, squeezed her hands and released her. "You're sure?"

Grace patted her belly. "Oh, yes." Her dragon left her in no doubt. The first place readied was the hatching grounds. Nervous, her dragon assured her not to worry. In a couple of weeks, she'd lay her eggs once the grounds got to the proper temperature.

It still drove her crazy, knowing she carried eggs within her.

Rog just laughed like a hyena when she mentioned that to him, then started his chicken dance before swinging her around. His smooching on her turned her indignance into giggles.

Grace watched Lavinia walk away, a bounce in her steps. She looked at Rog, her heart rapidly beating, her blood surging. The love in his eyes she would never take for granted.

"I love you." He knew the way to her heart.

But she knew his, too. "I love you."

Two halves of a whole. A dragon and his fated mate.

THE END

Books by Beverly

A Dragon's Fated Heart Series

Rise of the Dragons

Stealing Hope

Finding Faith

Saving Grace

The Santiago's Series

A Saint's Salvation

A Sailor's Delight

The Glen Series

Lightning Strike

Willow's Cry

Stand Alones

Dragons' Mate

Touched by the Sandman

A Dragon's Treasure

Triple D Dude Ranch

Love Me Forever

Anthologies

Destiny Whispers

We Know the Truth, Do you?

Take Two (July 2020)

Author Biography

Beverly Ovalle dabbled with writing on and off for years when her best friend finally dared her to submit a story to a writing contest. Beverly decided she had nothing to lose and since she'd always wanted to be an author sent it in and agonized for months waiting to hear back. Contract in hand she has never looked back.

Beverly has been obsessed with dragons and romance since she was a young girl, collecting dragon books and reading everything she could find on them even down to the care of real-life dragons. She's always been slightly panicked that the world as we know it will end, so has prepped for it, haunting survivalist pages and prepper projects she felt she needed in the event SHTF.

An avid fan of all romance, Beverly's goal is to share her love of the written word and write the hot and erotic romances that she enjoys. She writes what she loves to read and it was only a matter of time before her obsessions crept into her writing for her to share. She hopes you enjoy her tales as much as she loves writing them.

A Navy Veteran, Beverly has traveled around the world and the United States enabling her to bring her settings to life. Reading romances since the fourth grade she's followed as the genre changed and spread into the vast cornucopia of romance offered today.